William Earl Johns \
He served as a machine-{ -₋ı, and
from 1918 as a fighter pı -- ͻtayed with the
RAF until 1931 as a flight ı -uctor and a recruiting officer.
W E Johns started his civilian career as a skilful aviation artist and illustrator for magazines and books. When he became a writer, he added 'Captain' to his name. In the early 1930s he created his most famous hero, James Bigglesworth – 'Biggles'. Based on his own war experiences, Johns' character was an immediate success and he became an immensely popular boys' hero. In all, W E Johns wrote ninety-eight Biggles books, but he was also a successful writer of other novels and non-fiction. Due to the success of Biggles, he was asked by the Air Ministry to create a female pilot to stimulate recruitment to the WAAF, so he invented another character, 'Worrals'.

W E Johns died in 1968.

BY THE SAME AUTHOR
ALL PUBLISHED BY HOUSE OF STRATUS

Biggles and the Missing Millionaire
Biggles and the Pirate Treasure
Biggles and the Plane that Disappeared
Biggles Breaks the Silence
Biggles Flies to Work
Biggles Gets his Men
Biggles Looks Back
Biggles Makes Ends Meet
Biggles of the Interpol
Biggles of the Special Air Police
Biggles on Mystery Island
Biggles on the Home Front
Biggles Scores a Bull
Biggles Sees Too Much
Biggles Sets a Trap
Biggles Sorts It Out
Biggles Takes a Hand
Biggles Takes a Holiday
Biggles Takes Charge
Biggles Takes It Rough
Biggles Takes the Case
Biggles' Special Case
Boy Biggles
No Rest For Biggles

WORKS IT OUT

W E Johns

This edition published in 2001 by House of Stratus, an imprint of House of Stratus Ltd, Thirsk Industrial Park, York Road, Thirsk, North Yorkshire, YO7 3BX, UK.
Also at: House of Stratus Inc., 2 Neptune Road, Poughkeepsie, NY 12601, USA.

www.houseofstratus.com

Typeset, printed and bound by House of Stratus.

A catalogue record for this book is available from the British Library and The Library of Congress.

ISBN 0-7551-0734-9

CONTENTS

1	BIGGLES HAS SOMETHING TO SAY	1
2	A FRENCHMAN SETS A POSER	13
3	MODERN DAYS, MODERN WAYS	23
4	THE TRAIL TAKES SHAPE	32
5	INVESTIGATIONS	43
6	A MAN MINUS A BUTTON	53
7	MORE PROBLEMS	63
8	BERTIE TAKES A JOB	76
9	ALGY LEARNS THE ANSWERS	86
10	A TRIP TO REMEMBER	99
11	EL ASILE	110
12	BIGGLES TAKES A TURN	125
13	SMOKE IN THE SAHARA	133
14	ENEMIES OR ALLIES?	144
15	THE SUN DICTATES	155
16	WHERE THE TRAILS ENDED	167

1

BIGGLES HAS SOMETHING TO SAY

A cold east wind blustered across the home airport of the Special Air Police, bringing with it ragged curtains of trailing nimbus cloud that dripped their contents in a dreary drizzle on the shining concrete runways.

From the window of the Operations Room, Air Constable 'Ginger' Hebblethwaite watched without real interest the blurred silhouette of a departing continental 'Constellation'. Algy Lacey sat hunched in a chair near the stove, turning the pages of the current issue of *Flight*. Bertie Lissie, with his feet on a corner of the table, yawned audibly as with a circular movement that had become mechanical he polished his rimless eyeglass. Biggles sat at his desk, chin resting on the back of his left hand as with the other he turned over one by one a collection of newspaper clippings. A slender spiral of cigarette smoke made its way towards the ceiling from a cylinder head that served as an ashtray.

He had been silent for so long that Ginger's curiosity eventually wore out his patience. 'What's on your mind?' he asked.

Biggles lifted his cigarette and flicked the ash off as he looked up. 'Natural history,' he answered simply.

Ginger's expression turned slowly to one of questioning incredulity. 'What did you say?'

'I said,' replied Biggles evenly, 'I was thinking about natural history – or in terms of it, anyway.'

'Birds, beasts, butterflies, and all that sort of thing,' murmured Bertie.

'Exactly; but beasts, mostly,' Biggles told him.

'What about 'em, old boy?' queried Bertie. 'Tell us. This disgusting weather is binding me rigid. I mean to say, don't let the jolly old beasts get you down. I know how it feels. When I was a kid I used to dream a tiger was after me. There I was, all alone, no gun, nowhere to go, not even a bally tree to climb, with the horrid brute, all teeth and hair, getting closer and closer till I could feel its hot breath on my – '

'Okay – okay,' broke in Biggles impatiently. 'What are you trying to do – give yourself a nervous breakdown? I gather it never caught you?'

'Not quite. I always woke up just in time.'

Biggles sighed. 'What a pity.'

Bertie looked hurt. 'I take a dim view of that remark,' he protested. 'What do you mean – a pity?'

'Well, if it had got its teeth into your neck you could have relieved the tedium by telling us how it felt to be a tiger's breakfast.'

Algy stepped in. 'If you two are trying to convulse me with mirth you're nowhere near it,' he said coldly. 'What is all this rot about beasts anyhow?'

'Do you really want me to tell you?' inquired Biggles.

'Go ahead,' prompted Ginger. 'This place is getting the atmosphere of an overcrowded mortuary.'

'All right,' agreed Biggles. 'Here we go. Those of you who know anything about natural history may have noticed that as civilization advances across the wide-open spaces, the most dangerous beasts retire before it. That is to say, those that refuse to behave themselves must either submit to captivity or retreat to some inaccessible spot where they are reasonably safe from pursuit. Were they content to remain there no one would worry them; but they aren't; they want it both ways. Sooner or later they start making raids on the domestic animals that have taken their places on the ground which, on account of their unpleasant natures, they themselves have been forced to vacate.'

'By Jove! That's good,' declared Bertie admiringly. 'You talk like a book.'

Biggles' expression did not change. 'Let us for a moment say I am a book,' he agreed. 'Don't interrupt, or I shall forget where I was.'

'Sorry old boy – and all that,' murmured Bertie apologetically.

Biggles continued. 'The example of the wild beasts has been followed by a species of human being, and I don't necessarily mean native races. Most of those have now been tamed, although there are still a few that, having retired to a distance, by means of fast horses or camels play a merry game of tip and run with their hard-working brothers of the plains. We've seen this in Iraq and the North-west Frontier.'

'Hold hard a minute,' requested Algy. 'What has all this to do with us?'

'I'll come to that if you'll give me time,' complained Biggles. 'This is the point. I have a suspicion that the same game is being played by a certain type of man, supposed to be civilized, but who is still, under his skin, a beast of prey. Refusing to work like other fellows, he tries to live the easy way by toting a cosh and raiding the property of respectable folk. He doesn't take livestock or grain. They're too cumbersome. Gold, cash, and precious stones are the meat he seeks.'

'Is there anything new about this?' queried Algy.

'Unfortunately for us, yes,' replied Biggles. 'Finding the cities too hot to hold them, these well-dressed savages have, I fancy, retired to a distance where they are safe from pursuit, yet from where they can still help themselves to the property of the civilized communities. They don't use horses. They would be too slow, and the distances to be covered too great. It's my guess they are using the fastest means of transportation yet devised – the aeroplane.'

'You really think this is going on?' put in Ginger.

'I haven't the slightest doubt about it,' returned Biggles. 'It's the only answer to some of the clippings I have here. After all, why not? Why need a crook remain near the scene of his crime, when between sunset and dawn he can put himself five thousand miles away?'

No one answered.

'Unfortunately for him there's one snag in his scheme,' continued Biggles. 'When his aircraft isn't in use he can tuck it in a hide-out far away where it's not likely to be seen; but – and this is the point – when he makes a raid he must park it on the ground somewhere near the scene of the operation. That's his danger. When a farmer finds a fox is raiding his hen-roost he sets a trap, and the fox, wily though he may be, sooner or later puts his foot in it.'

'Not always,' disputed Bertie. 'There's an old dog fox on my place that has been going strong for years.'

'That's because you aren't smart enough to bag him,' argued Biggles.

'This old stinker knows the names of the people who make the traps,' asserted Bertie. 'He costs the Hunt a pretty penny in compensation for the poultry he snaffles, I can tell you.'

'All right. In that case it's your job to track him to his earth and winkle him out of it,' averred Biggles.

Algy stepped in again. Looking at Biggles he inquired: 'Has some particular incident started this fascinating train of thought?'

Biggles stubbed his cigarette. 'There have been several incidents lately that have made me suspect that at least one big-thinking, high-flying crook is on the job.'

'Air-operating costs being what they are, I'd question if a crooked aviation set-up of any size could pay its way,' opined Algy.

'And I'd say you'd be wrong,' answered Biggles. 'I'm not thinking in terms of picking pockets or robbing the till. Small-time crime will always go on; but real big-scale criminal operations are on the way, if they're not already here. Since Hitler upset the European apple-cart some of the clever boys must have made fortunes out of the economic situation – gold traffic, currency rackets, transporting war stores to prohibited areas, and so on. On one occasion a whole flight of Lancasters, worth forty thousand apiece, disappeared into the thinnest of thin air. The bright lads who pulled that off don't think in fivers. They think in millions. But times are changing, and those particular swindles are coming to an end. What are these fellows going to do? Retire from business? Change their ways? Scrap organizations that have taken years to build? Not on your life! Easy money soon goes. When it's gone they'll need more.'

'Governments are tightening things up,' reminded Algy.

'The clever crooks will always be a jump ahead,' declared Biggles. 'After all, what can the ordinary police do?'

'Too true – too true,' murmured Bertie thoughtfully. 'It's one thing to be a cop on the old home beat, but a nag of a different colour when you have the whole bally world to cover.'

'Maybe we're lucky at that,' opined Biggles. 'The day will come when there will have to be an Interplanetary Police

Force, with headquarters on the moon, to cover the whole blooming universe. But let's stick to the present. Let us suppose that we are crooks with plenty of money in the kitty. What hope would anyone have of catching us?'

Ginger looked interested. 'Go on,' he invited curiously. 'What would you do?'

Biggles took another cigarette and tapped the end pensively. 'First, I'd find a remote abandoned airstrip for a hide-out. That shouldn't be difficult, because thanks to the war every continent is littered with them. I might decide on several, widely separated. With a long-range aircraft I could hop from one to the other at will. I should have no big pay-load to carry, like commercial machines, so I should have plenty of extra tankage – enough say, for ten thousand miles.'

'What would you use for petrol?' inquired Algy cynically.

'With plenty of money we shouldn't have to worry about that,' stated Biggles. 'Enough money will buy anything – even a tanker full of hundred-octane aviation spirit. Thus equipped, with our own mechanics, who could catch us? We might be anywhere on earth, hopping from continent to continent overnight. An organization capable of dealing with us would cost millions. It would mean air-police patrols and control stations all over the globe. Even supposing I was seen, what could the police do? Police can stop a car on the road and look inside, but you can't stop an aircraft in the atmosphere and ask the pilot for his licence.'

'You can follow it,' contended Ginger.

'How far would depend on the fuel capacity of the pursuit plane. As a smart guy, I should see to it that my machine could outfly anything that the police had.'

'The police patrol could radio the next station to pick you up,' persisted Ginger.

'That's assuming I'm travelling in broad daylight with perfect visibility,' countered Biggles. 'Knowing where the police controls were, I should keep clear of them, anyway.'

'What about radar?'

'The police would need thousands of control stations to cover the globe, and since most governments are broke, no one would dare to vote the money for such a scheme.'

Algy shook his head. 'You'd need an awful lot of money to pay for a crook outfit on the lines you're suggesting.'

Biggles smiled. 'I should have a lot of money – while the going was good,' he declared. 'Unless I've missed my guess, some of the coups the big crooks have brought off lately have been more in the nature of wartime operations than mere bank busting or bag snatching. That's why I'm sure aviation must come into the picture. The old-fashioned highwayman has become a skywayman in a big way. To be more specific, I fancy the bush-ranger has become a cloud-ranger.'

'What exactly do you mean by that?' inquired Ginger.

Biggles turned over the clippings on his desk and selected one. 'I'm thinking about this business in Australia the other day. Here, broadly speaking, is the story. Apparently there exists in the outback of the Northern Territory a smallish gold-mining concern that has been operating for some time with a good deal of success. Its name is Barula Creek. Owing to its output it has had a lot of publicity in the newspapers, which may have been responsible for what has happened there. As the mine is a long way from anywhere, the gold is transferred to Port Darwin, about three hundred miles away, four times a year. Later, it goes to Sydney – but we needn't bother with that. For the overland journey, from the mine to Darwin, two jeeps are used. Apparently the country is rough, with some areas of desert. There's no real road. The personnel of the convoy consists of two driver mechanics, a spare driver, and two guards, all armed. That's five men all together; enough, it was thought, to deal with any trouble. The last convoy left Barula Creek just over a fortnight ago carrying nearly half a ton of gold. It didn't arrive. When a search party went to look for it they found a wrecked jeep, a damaged jeep, and five dead men. The leading jeep had been blown to bits either by a mine or a bomb. The gold had gone. Black trackers were brought in. They found some footmarks – but nothing else.'

'If there were footprints they would lead somewhere,' interposed Ginger.

'In this case they didn't. They ran for some way into an open desert area and then faded out. As one of the reporters put it, the murderers might have dropped from the sky. That may be nearer the literal truth than he imagined.'

'If an aircraft had landed there, there would have been wheel tracks,' put in Algy.

'Not necessarily. A machine can obliterate its tracks in dusty ground by its own slipstream.'

'How about going out and having a look round?' suggested Bertie hopefully. 'Be an excuse for getting out of this foul weather – if you see what I mean?'

'If native trackers couldn't find anything, it's unlikely that we should,' answered Biggles dryly. 'Still, one never knows. Native trackers wouldn't be thinking in terms of aviation. I might speak to Raymond. He could contact the authorities in Australia to see how they felt about it. This is an international, rather than a national, affair.'

'Why are you so sure an aircraft was used for the job?' asked Algy.

'To my mind it sticks out like a sore finger,' returned Biggles. 'How was the stolen gold carried? The robbers wouldn't be likely to carry half a ton of gold on their backs across hundred of miles of waterless country. A vehicle must have been used, and any vehicle except an aircraft would have left tracks that an aboriginal could follow, no matter how carefully they were covered up. I say this was a carefully planned raid by men who had at least one big aircraft and knew how to handle it. As soon as the robbery was discovered the police threw a net round the whole area. When it was pulled tight there was nothing in it.' Biggles smiled grimly. 'By that time the birds had not only flown, but were probably roosting quietly thousands of miles away.'

'But surely an aircraft would have been seen by somebody?' said Ginger.

'One would think so. But Australia is a big country,' reminded Biggles. 'Moreover, if the raiders were as clever as they seem to have been, they would have climbed to the ceiling, where they would not have been noticed. Or, since they had no reason to hurry, they could have waited for darkness before hitting the breeze.'

'There can't be many men able to pull off a job like that,' observed Algy.

Biggles shrugged. 'It wouldn't be difficult for a man who during the war was on Special Air Service operations over enemy country. We've handled more difficult briefs ourselves if it comes to that. But for the murders I should have said it was a nice clean job.'

'Why murder the guards, anyway?' muttered Ginger.

'In my view they were murdered simply and solely to prevent them from saying how the job was done. The longer these crooks can work without anyone suspecting the employment of an aircraft, so much the easier for them.'

'They must be a bunch of thugs,' growled Bertie.

'The modern thug can be a very charming fellow when he's not working,' said Biggles softly.

'One would think that a fellow capable of organizing an air operation on such a scale would be able to earn a comfortable living without turning to crime,' opined Algy.

Biggles shook his head. 'The trouble is, too many chaps don't want a comfortable job. They may not even need money. What they really crave is excitement. It may be fun at first, but the humour gets a bit thin when the hangman rolls up with his rope. That's how these frolics usually end. At the best, I'd hate to spend ten years of my life in the same cell staring at the same bit of sky through a barred window. Once a fellow gets out of step it isn't easy to pick it up again. He becomes a social misfit, drifting about without an anchor, mistrusting his so-called friends, never knowing when a heavy hand is going to drop on his shoulder. What a life! Our old friend Erich von Stalhein is a good example. He's got all it takes to put him on top of any profession: but it's too late. He knows that. He knows he's off the rails, and it's really anger at his own folly that makes him hate everyone who's on the level. That's why we keep bumping into each other. At the finish either he'll kill me or I shall kill him, because he'd rather die than go to jail. He might well be in this Australian affair. It's right up his street. If that is so he knows it can only be a matter of time before I strike his trail.' Biggles stubbed his cigarette.

'Have there been any robberies similar to this Australian affair?' inquired Algy.

'One, at least. I was checking these clippings for such possibilities. There was a queer business in Bolivia a couple of months ago. In that case an emerald mine was raided, apparently with the same success, although I haven't the details.'

Ginger's eyebrows went up. 'Bolivia! That's in South America. Even if an aircraft was used it could hardly have been the same one that did the job in Australia.'

'Why not?' questioned Biggles. 'As a matter of fact, we have now arrived at the crux of the debate. This is the angle I was considering when you first butted in. There is no actual reason to suppose that the robbery in Bolivia has any connection with the Australian affair; but if aircraft were used there's no reason why the same gang shouldn't have done both jobs. If that did turn out to be the case, maybe the government would get an idea of what the police are now up against.'

'Are you going to do anything about it?' inquired Ginger.

'No, but I shall discuss the matter with the Air Commodore in order to be able to move fast should anything of this sort occur nearer home. One thing is certain. Someone will soon have to do something if these raids go on, because robberies on such a scale can upset the entire economy of a country. No government can afford to lose half a ton of gold.'

'But what can be done about it, old boy?' put in Bertie.

'Very little, unless the nations threatened get together and show a more co-operative spirit than they do at present.'

'What about the International Police Commission?' reminded Ginger.

Biggles shrugged. 'It's a capital idea. In theory it looks fine. But how far does it go in practice? About as far as the rest of the international organizations. Countries are still working on their own, just as we are. That's no use. To make the thing efficient every country should have its air police. All should be constantly in touch to exchange views and information. Look at us. I suppose we're part of this commission, but how often do we see any foreign members?'

'Have you ever suggested a general meeting?' asked Ginger.

'Several times. Nothing came of it.'

'Well, what are you going to do?'

'For the moment, nothing. It's no use tearing about the atmosphere without knowing what we're looking for.'

Ginger moved nearer to the window as from the murk came the sound of an aircraft feeling its way in. 'I hope he's enjoying himself,' he murmured cynically. There was a short pause before he went on. 'He's down all right. Looks like a Frenchman – a military Morane with civil markings.'

Nobody paid much attention. But when, presently, Ginger remarked, 'The pilot's coming this way,' Biggles looked interested.

'Who is it?' he asked.

'Search me. I've never seen him before. Yes, he's coming here. The Flight Sergeant has pointed out the office.'

A minute later there came a knock on the door, which was opened to admit a dapper young man in well-worn flying-kit. He glanced from one to the other, smiling. 'Good morning, sirs,' he said cheerfully.

'Good morning to you,' returned Biggles. 'What can I do for you? Take a seat. Have a cigarette?'

2

A FRENCHMAN SETS A POSER

The stranger accepted the chair Ginger pulled forward, and a cigarette. 'Your weather I do not like,' he said, as he clicked his lighter.

'We don't like it ourselves,' replied Biggles. 'But as it's dished out to us we have to take it as it comes. Forgive me if I appear abrupt, but is that what you came to talk about?'

'No – no,' was the quick reply. 'But tell me this. Do I speak with Capitaine Bigglesworth?'

'You do – if you speak to me,' returned Biggles.

'Good. Now we talk at last some business,' said the visitor, with warm satisfaction in his voice.

'What business?' asked Biggles, looking a trifle surprised.

'Police business. Ah! Forgive me; I am a fool; I forget; you do not know me. I am Marcel Brissac, the French Air Police.'

'Just you?' Biggles smiled.

'*Oui, monsieur*. Just me. La, la! So you are the famous Beegles?'

Bertie adjusted his eyeglass. 'Here, just a minute, old top. In this country beagles are dogs, you know.'

The French pilot laughed. '*Bon*. So he is an old dog. He shows me some tricks, perhaps?'

Biggles' smile broadened. 'Perhaps we can show each other some. By the way, a long time ago, in France, I knew a *pilote de chasse* of your name. His name was Charles Brissac, of the *Escadrille Cigognes*. Was he a relation of yours?'

'A relation? *Tiens!* He is my father, and to you he sends his felicitations, *monsieur*,' answered Marcel.

'Is he still flying?'

'No. A little while ago, yes. But now he is *Administrateur* of the *Direction de la Navigation Aerienne*. I am a Capitaine of the *Armée de l'Air*, but I am selected for the duty special of catching flying *voleurs* – how do you call them, thiefs?'

'Have you caught any?'

Marcel shrugged. 'Not one. This makes me sad, and it is my father who says to me go to England and make correspondence with Beeglesworth. So here I come.'

Biggles glanced round the room. 'This is odd, after what I was saying just now. It looks as if there's going to be a little real co-operation at last.'

First impressions are not necessarily infallible; but they are important, and usually to be trusted. Ginger liked Marcel Brissac on sight. He was so obviously alive, and so glad to be alive. His vitality revealed itself in every eloquent gesture that he made – and he made many. Enthusiasm and good humour sparkled in his dark eyes when he spoke; and there were moments when words fairly rattled off his lips in his anxiety to give expression to his thoughts. Indeed, there were times when his exuberance, which he made no attempt to conceal, made Ginger laugh, because it was so obviously genuine. Every passing emotion was reflected instantly on his face.

He was, Ginger judged, about twenty-five, slim, with fine, clean-cut features and a miniature black moustache decorating his upper lip. His general appearance was neat, without being foppish. Above all he was natural, plainly –

and sensibly – seeing no reason to be otherwise. In a word, he was just as typically French as Biggles was British. Later it was learned that during the war he had served with the Free French Air Force, which accounted for his knowledge of English, which was sound, even if his choice of words was sometimes whimsical.

Biggles was speaking. 'Tell me, Marcel; has anything happened in your department? I mean, was there any special incident on which you wanted my opinion?'

'Does something happen?!' cried Marcel. 'Something happens all the time. These thiefs...how do you call them?'

'Crooks.'

'Ah, yes. These crooks who fly are busy. It is to stop them I am ordered.'

Biggles' eyes twinkled. 'How are you going to do that?'

Marcel threw up his hands helplessly. 'You ask me? I come here to ask you.'

'If I knew where to start I wouldn't be sitting here,' Biggles pointed out.

'Perhaps together we can find them,' suggested Marcel hopefully.

'We can try,' conceded Biggles. 'Have you anything to work on? We have nothing here.'

'Wait! I show you something,' declared Marcel earnestly. He took a notebook from his breast pocket. Selecting a sheet of paper, he unfolded it and put it on the desk. 'Perhaps this means something, perhaps not. I do not know. Have you seen this aeroplane?' He tapped the paper with an energetic forefinger.

The others crowded round to look. On the paper was a rough sketch of an aircraft – to be precise a Douglas DC3, although certain slight modifications appeared to have been made to it.

'What is this supposed to be?' asked Biggles, looking up.

'This is what I ask you, monsieur,' returned Marcel.

Biggles looked again at the sketch. 'I don't see anything remarkable about it,' he went on. 'This aircraft is, or was, a Douglas DC3, although it might have been converted for some special job. It seems to have been fitted with a tricycle under-carriage. That, to some extent, makes it unique. The DC4 has a tricycle undercarriage, but that's a four-engined job. This is a twin. What about the machine, anyway?'*

'This is a picture given to me by my friend Paul Legendre, of the service Air France,' explained Marcel. 'There is something strange about it. I will tell you. My friend Paul works on the African service, between Gao, in the French Sudan, and Algiers. The ground is very bad, always desert the most terrible all the way. In the middle are the Ahaggar Mountains, where no man goes, except sometimes the most savage Arabs. One day not many weeks ago Paul is flying up from Gao. He meets the thing he always dreads, the storm of sand. Up he takes himself to get over it. But no! It is not possible. But on high it is not so bad as low down, you understand? Suddenly there passes close by him an aeroplane. He stares. Is this possible? he asks himself. No, no. Is it his shadow? No. There is no sun to make shadows. Besides it is on a course for the middle of the Sahara. It is not like his own, although it carries the letter F of France. He makes a picture of it on his brain. Then it goes, and he sees it no more. This is the story he tells me in Paris, in the *Aero Club de France*.

* The twin-engined Douglas DC3 is one of the most universally used transports. A low-wing cantilever monoplane, it takes many forms and has many names. In the American army one type was known as the Skytrain. Another type was the Skytrooper. In the US Navy it was the R.40-I. As supplied to the RAF it was the Dakota I and Dakota 2. The engines were either 'Wasps' or 'Cyclones' driving three-bladed airscrews. The Skytrain would carry twenty-eight troops complete with equipment.

Because he is an artist he makes of this aeroplane a picture, which is what I show you now.' Marcel tapped the sketch.

'Is Paul still on the same run?' asked Biggles.

'Yes.'

'Has he seen the plane again?'

'No. Always he looks, but there is nothing but sand, and in the distance, the Mountains of the Ahaggar. But wait! When he tells this story in Paris there are in the club many pilots. One is named Georges Pinsard. He also is of Air France, of the service *Transatlantique*, to New York by way of Azores. He looks at this picture. Very strange, he says. I also have seen this machine, over the sea four hours out from Paris. Name of a name! cried Georges. I have a shock when it springs out of the clouds and passes so close that if I do not make a sudden turn we must meet face to face. But Paul, says Georges, you make a mistake. This machine is not of France. When I see it, it carries the letters CS of Portugal. No, no, says Paul. I will swear it carries the letter F. But, says Georges, how can it carry the registration letter F when there is no machine of that type in the French service? That is true. I know it.' Marcel looked at Biggles and shrugged his shoulders. 'You see? Here is a machine that no one knows and belongs to two countries. Is there something – how do you say? – fishy, about that?'

'Very fishy,' murmured Biggles slowly, staring at the sketch. 'I don't know that particular machine, and it's my business to know most things with wings. When Georges saw this machine, and apparently nearly collided with it, he was, you say, four hours out from Paris?'

'Yes.'

'Then the machine was on its way to Europe?'

'To Europe or North Africa. Its course was a little south of east.'

Biggles took a cigarette and tapped it thoughtfully. 'Very interesting,' he said. 'Very interesting indeed.' Looking up at Marcel, he went on, 'Did either of these pilots, Paul or Georges, mention the matter to the control officer when they got in?'

'But of course,' was the emphatic answer. 'They must put it in their flight reports. I have examined these with my father. We make much of the affair because this is how accidents are made.'

'What had the control officer to say of this?'

'What can he say when he knows nothing? I ask if Air France has such a machine, a new one perhaps. He says no. I ask the Portuguese Attaché in Paris if he has such a machine. He says Portugal has no machine like it.'

'Big machines are usually in touch with the airfield of their arrival or departure, but this one seems to have been a lone wolf, in touch with nobody.'

'It sent no signals,' declared Marcel. 'I have examined the control records of the days when it was seen.'

'That isn't to say that the machine didn't receive signals,' put in Algy. 'It could have picked up weather reports while keeping wireless silence itself.'

'It could have been in touch with its base on a special wavelength, if it comes to that,' asserted Biggles. 'What about when it was over Central Africa, heading, apparently, for the middle of the Sahara – in a sandstorm with visibility, at ground level, nil? It rather looks as if that pilot knew where he was going. We must suppose he was in touch with somebody, or he'd have been heading out of the murk, not farther into it. It all boils down to this. Here is an aircraft that carries French or Portuguese markings when it suits it, but is known to neither country. No machine on legitimate business would behave like that. It was, therefore, on business of its own; and, it seems, changes its registration marking to suit itself. If it has worn both French and Portuguese markings it has probably worn others. It would have to carry markings of some sort in case it was seen. A complete absence of markings, military or civil, would be noticed by another pilot. Observe that the markings, when they were seen, were appropriate to the position. When the machine was over French territory it carried F. Between the Azores and Europe, as the Azores are Portuguese, it carried CS. I am well aware that there have for some time been one or two small machines dodging about, particularly at night, on questionable business; but this is something bigger. Here we have a big machine that obviously has a range of thousands of miles. Well, I can't say I'm particularly surprised.'

'We must catch this machine and find out its business,' declared Marcel.

'I'm with you there, but how do you suggest we start?' asked Biggles. 'This machine may be on the ground for weeks at a time. To start patrolling the sky aimlessly in the hope of seeing it would be like looking for a flea in a fur coat. Never mind, Marcel. You have at least produced a clue, which is something we hadn't got when you drifted in. More important still, I'm glad to know that France is willing to co-operate with us in a practical way. Between us we should be able to catch up with this wily aviator who seems to be playing the old pirate trick of changing his colours when it suits him.'

'We certainly ought to be able to trace a machine of that size,' put in Algy. 'The company that sold it, new or second-hand, is bound to have a record of the sale.'

'One would think so,' agreed Biggles. 'But don't overlook the fact that more than one air-operating company has gone out of business without accounting for its aircraft. Apart from that, more aircraft have disappeared without trace than is generally realized. The Avro Tudor, named the Star Tiger, disappeared in January 1949, and a sister ship, the Star Aerial, shortly afterwards. You may remember the fuss that resulted in an inquiry? I can think offhand of nine big machines, including at least one DC3, that went out and never came back. All we know about them is they disappeared without trace. In one case, I recall, an American committee of experts reckoned that someone had tinkered with the fire-extinguishing apparatus, releasing carbon dioxide which gassed the crew and the passengers. But that was only surmise.'

'What you're really saying is, one or more of these machines may not in fact have crashed at all?' put in Ginger.

'Since Marcel produced his picture of a DC3 which seems to have queer habits, it has occurred to me that at least one of these missing machines might still be airworthy,' admitted Biggles. 'It's unlikely, but possible.'

'In other words,' suggested Ginger, 'someone may have pinched a machine?'

'If so, it wouldn't be the first machine to be taken up by an unauthorized person – off its own airfield at that. When you think of it, what could be easier to steal than an aircraft, even a big passenger job, by someone who could fly?'

'Here, wait a minute old boy,' objected Bertie. 'I don't quite get that.'

'All right. Let us go back to the argument that we four are crooks. A fellow comes along and says, I'll give you ten thousand pounds for a Douglas, delivered to my private airfield in Central Africa. We decide to accept. All right. With guns in our pockets we book as ordinary passengers. No one is to know we can fly. When we're in the air Ginger knocks the radio operator on the head and takes over signals. I do the same with the pilot. Algy and Bertie deal with the rest of the crew. What could the passengers do about it? Nothing. They'd be too scared to move. Later they could be disposed of in any way that suited us. Ginger sends out an SOS that the machine is on fire and we're coming down in the Bay of Biscay or somewhere. Search parties rush to the spot. What do they find? Nothing. Why? Because the plane, in perfectly good order, is on the ground a thousand miles away, having been delivered to the man who wanted it. We share out the ten thousand and come home in our own time, or, maybe, go on working for our crooked employer.'

Marcel's eyes were nearly popping out of his head. '*Mon Dieu!*' he cried. 'It is a good thing for aviation that you are the police, and not crooks.'

'What we could do other people could do,' asserted Biggles, smiling. 'My point is, it could happen.'

'How about getting down to facts?' put in Algy. 'This mystery plane that Marcel has provided – what are you going to do about it?'

Biggles lit another cigarette. 'As far as I can see there's only one thing we can do at the moment, and that is check up on all DC3s that have vanished without trace. We might at the same time ascertain the names of the people on board, both crew and passengers. That would tell us whether the aircraft was simply on test or working on a scheduled flight. I'm certainly not going to fly up and down the Sahara or round and round the Atlantic on the off chance of meeting Marcel's mystery kite. The Sahara isn't our territory, anyway.' Biggles thought for a moment, then looked at his French colleague. 'I'm going to speak to my chief about this,' he said. 'Meanwhile, Marcel, you might make some discreet inquiries about that area of the Sahara where the Douglas was seen. France has both civil and service machines flying in that part of the world. I suggest you make a round of the aerodromes and find out if any of your pilots have noticed a place where a big machine could lie low without being fried to a cinder by the sun.'

Marcel looked dubious. 'The heat,' he averred, 'is formidable.'

'I know that,' answered Biggles. 'But after all, this mystery kite that flies false colours has to land somewhere. It may have been making for its hide-out when it was seen over the Sahara. It might have been making for the same place when it was seen over the Atlantic, if it comes to that. Its course would be about right. One thing we can be sure of,' he concluded. 'The pilot wasn't digging his way through that dust storm towards the Ahaggar Mountains for the fun of it.'

'That is true,' agreed Marcel seriously. 'I will go to Africa. When I have something to tell you I come back.'

Biggles got up. 'Okay. If that's settled let's go over to the canteen and see what they can produce in the way of lunch.'

3

MODERN DAYS, MODERN WAYS

The Air Police Wellington roared a challenge to Nature in the rough as its engines kicked the air behind them five thousand feet above a patchwork quilt of light and shade, of rock and sand, of withered salt-bush and purple scrub, that comprises most of the landscape where the Great Sandy Desert of Australia rubs shoulders with the Northern Territory. From time to time, between sun-cracked hills, some of which were craters of long-dead volcanoes, rivers spilled themselves on wide, stony flats; but they were rivers of sand. The water that once had filled their beds had long ago departed, no man knew when, or where, or how. Above, from a vacant sky, a relentless sun tormented a vacant land.

Nearly four hundred miles behind the tail of the aircraft as it headed south, on the coast of the Timor Sea, lay Port Darwin, its last port of call. Ahead, the monotonous panorama, marked only by an occasional fringe of gloomy pines, rolled on to a hopeless horizon, beyond which, somewhere, a scratch in the earth's crust had been named Barula Creek.

A fortnight had elapsed since the conversation at the Air Police Operational Headquarters, as a result of which, and a subsequent conference with Air Commodore Raymond at Scotland Yard, the journey to Australia had been undertaken. Biggles made no secret of the fact that he did not expect to find anything where Australia's celebrated black trackers had failed; but, as he averred, there was nothing to work on at home, so there could be no harm in trying. He had one or two cards up his sleeve, as will in due course be revealed.

The Air Commodore had been in touch with the Dominion Police, and having explained the possible international nature of the robbery, was invited to investigate on the spot if he thought it worthwhile. Algy, as Biggles' second-in-command, had remained at home ready to deal with a repetition of the affair should it occur, or fly to the support of Marcel should the French pilot strike a promising trail before the Australian expedition returned. Actually, it suited him to stay, because he had an appointment with his dentist.

'We ought to be getting close,' remarked Biggles to Ginger, who was sitting next to him, after a glance at the time. 'Keep your eyes open. With the landscape all looking alike we could overshoot the mine if we were slightly off our course. Is that something straight ahead or is it just another outcrop of rock?'

'I should say that's it,' returned Ginger, a minute later, as the object to which Biggles had called attention took on a more regular shape, and finally resolved itself into a cluster of buildings.

There was no need to look far for a landing-ground, for most of the country around the hutments that comprised the Barula Creek gold workings was flat and treeless. The creek that gave the place its name was presumably a dried-up river-bed that started in some distant mountains and lost itself in the desert near the mine. The buildings were more extensive than Ginger had thought they would be, and suggested that a fair number of people were employed at this remote enterprise.

Biggles landed without trouble, and after taxying nearer to the buildings, got out, the others with him, and walked the rest of the way. Two men were already coming to meet them. Both were tall, powerfully built and sunburnt, wearing drill breeches with open-necked shirts and broad-rimmed hats. They greeted the airmen in a friendly manner but with evident surprise.

'Where have you come from?' asked one.

'From England,' answered Biggles.

'That's a long way.'

'Planes fly a long way nowadays,' remarked Biggles, smiling. 'From what I've heard, it seems that highway robbers travel far and fast, too.'

'Is that what you've come about?'

'It is.'

'Come to the office and have a drink.'

'Thanks. It is pretty warm out here.'

On the way Biggles introduced himself and his companions. The mine officials returned the compliment. One, John Brand, was the manager, and the other, George Symonds, was his assistant. It turned out that they had had no warning of Biggles' mission. However, refreshments were produced, and they all sat in cane chairs on the office verandah to discuss the matter.

'Frankly, I don't expect to find much,' admitted Biggles.

'I shall be surprised if you find anything,' was the equally frank rejoinder.

'The only reason I came was this,' explained Biggles. 'We're not ordinary police investigators. We specialize on the air angle of crime, and there's just a chance that an aircraft was used to lift your gold. No doubt you've had expert trackers all over the ground, in which case, in the ordinary way, we should be flattering ourselves if we suggested that we might find something they'd missed. But they're not used to aircraft. We are. There are certain tricks of the trade, and we're properly equipped to deal with them. If I do no more than confirm that an aircraft was used for the robbery, my trip will have been worth while.'

Brand thumbed his pipe. 'I see. Well, we'll help you all we can. The man who can catch these crooks who shot my men is my friend for life.'

'How far are we from the place where the hold-up occurred?'

'Close on a hundred miles. The district is called Sandy Bottoms. You'll see nothing if you go there.'

'I'd like to see it, all the same,' returned Biggles. 'Would you mind showing it to me?'

'Sure I will. How do you reckon to get there?'

'Flying would be the quickest way, if there's somewhere handy to land.'

'There won't be any difficulty about that,' asserted Brand. 'There's all the room in the world.'

'That's fine. Then while we're having a breather you might tell me as much as you know about the affair,' suggested Biggles.

Brand puffed at his pipe. 'There isn't a lot to tell. We know how the job was done. Trackers soon worked that out. As you know, we used two jeeps to transport the gold, which was in the form of ingots. It's ideal country for them. The load was split between them. Five men made the trip, three in the first jeep, and two in the second. We didn't expect trouble. We'd never had any, but we believed in playing safe. The jeeps followed the usual track. At Sandy Bottoms there's a kind of knoll, with some scrub. The track skirts it. Here the leading jeep ran on a land mine. At least, that's what it looks like. I was in North Africa in the war, so I know what a mine can do. All three men in the jeep must have been killed outright. The second jeep pulled up. As the two men in it jumped out they were shot down by gunmen hidden in the scrub, about ten yards away. They hadn't a chance. According to my trackers, and they don't make mistakes, there were three gunmen. They all wore shoes soled with ribbed crêpe rubber, which made them look alike. That may have been to confuse trackers, but you can't fool a black boy. One was a tall man with a slight limp in his right leg. One was shorter and more heavily built, and the third was a little chap. There were plenty of tracks round the jeeps of course, because it took these fellows some time to shift the gold. But there was nothing else, not even a cartridge case; but we know that the bullets that killed our fellows were fired from .303 service rifles.'

'What became of the tracks?' asked Biggles. 'They must have led somewhere.'

'They faded out in the desert quite close to where the hold-up took place. After that the thieves might have taken wing and flown away for all the signs they left.'

'You may be right, at that,' said Biggles. 'We'll fly over presently and take a few vertical photographs of the area.'

Brand seemed surprised. 'What can photos show you that can't be seen with your own eyes on the ground?'

'Curiously enough, the camera can see what the eye can't see,' answered Biggles. 'It can see through sand, for instance. In Egypt the camera has located buried cities. At home it has pinpointed Roman camps under farm-lands, although there isn't a sign of them at ground level.'

'And what do you reckon your camera might see at Sandy Bottoms?' Brand was clearly sceptical.

'Tracks.'

'What sort of tracks?'

'Well, hardened wheel tracks, for instance.'

'Had there been any tracks my boys would have found them. Fresh-made tracks would be on top of the ground, not under it.'

'Not necessarily,' argued Biggles. 'An aircraft can kick up a cloud of dust which, when it settles, can smother everything.'

Brand sucked on his pipe. 'I didn't think of that.'

'At all events, there are wheel tracks there, that's certain,' asserted Biggles.

'Why certain?'

'Because I refuse to believe that three men, or even a dozen men, carried boxes containing half a ton of gold ingots on their backs, with the water they would require, out of that blistering desert I've just flown over. If you argue that it's just possible, then I say such a trip would take weeks, in which case someone would have seen these fellows. No, Brand, these men rode. If they rode they used a vehicle, and all vehicles have wheels, including aircraft. Even if they used pack-horses or mules there would still be tracks.'

'I guess you're right,' conceded Brand.

'There's one thing that puzzles me,' went on Biggles. 'These bandits didn't just park themselves in the desert on the off chance of a load of gold coming along. They knew when it was due. How did they know? Was the information made public?'

'No, although I can't say we took particular care to keep the date a secret,' replied Brand. 'We didn't advertise it, if that's what you mean.'

'Well, the bandits weren't guessing,' replied Biggles. 'I take it you can trust your staff?'

'Absolutely. It's months since any one of them left the mine, anyway. They get one holiday a year, when they go to Melbourne to see the Cup.'

'Have you had any visitors lately?'

Brand thought for a minute. 'I can only think of one. There was a chap dropped in, now you come to mention it. But he was a newspaper man, doing a story on the outback.'

'Who said so?'

'He did.'

'And you took his word for it?'

'Didn't seem to be any reason why I shouldn't.'

'How long ago was this?'

'Not long before the hold-up. I can't remember the actual date.'

'How did this chap arrive?'

'Same way as you, in an airplane.'

Biggles caught Ginger's eye. Then he looked back at Brand. 'Was he alone?'

'Yes.'

'I imagine he told you his name?'

'Sure he did. It was Canton – Dick Canton.'

'What sort of plane did he come in?'

'Couldn't say. I don't know anything about planes. It was only a little machine – had two seats. The colour was a sort of brownish green. I recall hearing one of my boys say it was an American make.'

'Where did this fellow come from, and where did he go when he left here?'

Brand frowned. 'In this part of the world we don't ask personal questions. We leave a fellow to tell us as much as he wants us to know.'

'It might be a good thing if you did ask a few questions, in future,' said Biggles dryly. 'I take it this chap was British?'

'He talked like a Britisher fresh from England – you know, a bit la-de-dah.'

Biggles smiled. 'How long did he stay here?'

'He came in the morning, had lunch with us, and left in the afternoon.'

'Was the gold mentioned?'

'Of course. That's what he came about. He wanted the facts for the story he was doing for his paper. I don't remember exactly what I told him. He spoke to other people besides me.'

'He could have learned that the gold was ready to be moved?'

'Of course. Are you suggesting – ?'

'I'm not suggesting anything, yet,' interposed Biggles. 'Like this visitor of yours, I'm just collecting all the facts I can while I'm here. What sort of fellow was he in appearance?'

'Towny type, blue suit an' all that. Height about five foot six roughly, thin, and very dark. I'd put his age about thirty-five. Had a little black moustache. Brushed his hair straight back without a parting, I remember. Said he did it to hide a wound in the head he got in the war. He was always fiddling with it.'

Biggles lit a cigarette. 'I find this all very interesting,' he said. 'When would it be convenient for you to fly over with me and have a look at Sandy Bottoms?'

'When do you want to go?'

'It would suit me to go now. The sun's practically overhead. That's the best angle for the photos I want.'

'Are you going to land?'

'Not yet. I don't want my own tracks to interfere with any on the ground. I'll get the photos and develop them first. We've brought the equipment.'

'All right, let's go,' agreed Brand, rising.

In a few minutes the machine was in the air again, heading north. Brand, sitting next to Biggles, pointed out the track taken by the jeeps, a thin, faint, wavy line that sometimes disappeared in scrub or on beds of shingle.

Half an hour later, cruising at five thousand feet, they arrived over the objective, plainly marked by the knoll and the shattered jeep at the base of it. The second jeep, Brand said, had been towed home. For the rest, the terrain was a sandy waste, spotted with saltbush, that had obviously given the place its name.

'There's one thing about this that doesn't fit with your idea,' remarked Brand.

'What is it?'

'If a plane was parked out there on the Bottoms the boys in the jeeps would have seen it when they came along.'

Biggles agreed. 'But,' he pointed out, 'they wouldn't have seen it had it been standing on the opposite side of the knoll. If it comes to that, the machine could have been a mile away when the hold-up took place. It could have been taxied to the spot afterwards.'

'You've always got the answer ready,' admitted Brand.

Biggles grinned. 'That's my job,' he averred, and then warned Ginger on the intercom to stand by. Under his instructions, as he made two parallel runs over the objective, Ginger exposed twelve plates. They then returned to the mine, and leaving Ginger and Bertie to develop the plates, Biggles went back with Brand to the verandah to continue the discussion until the prints were ready. Brand, with true Australian hospitality, insisted that they should all share his table while they were there.

4

THE TRAIL TAKES SHAPE

In due course Bertie appeared with the first prints. They were still wet. 'I think we've got something here, old boy,' he said briskly, putting the prints on the table and handing Biggles the magnifying glass. He pointed. 'If those aren't wheel tracks I'll eat the label in my hat. They're faint, and all that, but they're there.'

Biggles studied the picture intently. 'You're right,' he said slowly. 'Those are certainly wheel tracks – very interesting wheel tracks, too.' He looked up at Brand. 'Is there any possibility of anyone using a vehicle of any sort in the region of Sandy Bottoms, apart from your own jeeps?'

'Not the remotest,' declared Brand. 'I shouldn't think anyone since time began has taken a vehicle across Sandy Bottoms – except, of course, on the track. As far as I know, no one except ourselves ever used the track.'

Biggles handed him the magnifying glass. 'Take a look. You can see the marks. Did your trackers cover that ground?'

'I think so. They made casts all round the place. I was with them. Those tracks weren't there then, I'll swear, or they'd have seen them. But half a minute. That's a queer sort of track, isn't it? Looks like it was made by something with three wheels.'

'I rather fancy it was,' returned Biggles softly.

'The only thing I know with three wheels is a tricycle.'

'Most big aeroplanes have three wheels,' Biggles pointed out. 'Two landing-wheels and a tail wheel.'

'And you think this was made by one of them?'

'No, I don't, although it's just possible. Those three lines are absolutely parallel. Unless the machine made a perfect three-point landing and ran absolutely straight, the inside track, made by the tail wheel, would wobble a bit. Any slight obstruction would probably cause the middle line to wag a bit. The definition of the middle line would vary, too, as the machine touched down, before the weight became evenly distributed on all three wheels.'

Brand looked puzzled. 'Then what's the answer?'

'There's another sort of landing-gear which has two main wheels and a smaller one in front. It's known, technically, as a tricycle undercarriage, and that's precisely what it is. The even spacing of the tracks we're looking at incline me to the view that they were made by such a device. But this is something I can think about at leisure. We mustn't take up too much of your time. Let's go back. I know just where to land, now, in order to try the experiment I have in mind. We'll go as soon as we've had dinner, if that's okay with you? If you'd bring one of your trackers along I'd be glad.' Biggles smiled. 'We may even be able to show him something.'

'He'll soon spot those tracks.'

'Had they been visible he would have seen them when he was there,' said Biggles quietly. 'I shall land in line with them just where they fade out. Not that they'll be there for us to see, you understand? I fancy they're under the sand, not on it. I'm hoping I shall be able to expose them.'

'You mean, brush the loose sand off them?'

'Not brush it off – blow it off. You'll see.'

As soon as the meal was finished the aircraft headed back to the scene of the hold-up, Brand having with him his most experienced tracker, a shock-headed, wizened old aboriginal named Joe. Biggles took the greatest possible care over his landing, making three trial runs before touching down. Not a breath of air stirred, which enabled him to choose his direction. As soon as the machine had finished its run he turned it in its own length so that its tail pointed straight down the estimated position of the wheel tracks – estimated, because they were certainly not there to be seen. Leaving the engines running they all got down. To Brand, Biggles said: 'You saw the photo. Do you agree that we're now just about at the end of those tracks?'

Brand said he did.

'Well, where are the tracks?'

Brand tilted up his hat and scratched his head. 'They aren't there,' he said in a curious voice.

'Ask Joe if the sand we're looking at is packed hard, or fresh.'

Brand obliged. Joe knelt, touched the sand with his fingers, and smelt it. Bent double, he quartered the ground like a gun dog. Returning, he stated that the sand behind the aeroplane was loose.

'Good,' said Biggles. 'We'll see if we can move some of it. Bertie, get aboard and make some wind – not too much.'

Bertie climbed up. The engines growled. The sand began to creep, like a long trickle of water, here and there, making little whirlpools. As the noise increased to a roar a cloud of dust swirled aft into the thin air. As it did so a curious thing happened. Slowly there appeared on the ground three parallel lines, running across the arid earth, becoming fainter in the distance.

Biggles signalled to Bertie to cut the engines. 'There we are,' he said with satisfaction in his voice. 'I don't know any surface vehicle that makes a track as wide as that. It could only have been made by an aircraft, and a big one at that. Take the measurements, Ginger.'

Brand was staring like a man who has difficulty in believing what he sees. 'I thought I knew something about tracking, but that's a new one on me,' he muttered. 'What's Joe after?'

The black was running through the settling dust to intercept what appeared to be a small white butterfly that had been blown high into the air. It fell on a clump of saltbush. He picked it off with great care, came back, and showed what he held in the palm of his hand. It was a tiny piece of tissue paper, perhaps three inches long and a quarter of an inch wide. There was some printing on it in pale blue ink. Biggles took it, and turning it over revealed that it was in fact a tiny paper tube, sealed at both ends, although it had been torn across the middle.

'What the dickens is it?' asked Ginger in a mystified voice.

Biggles read the printing aloud. 'Favor-Paris. Cure-Dents Sterilisé. Hotel de Paris. MC.'

Brand looked at Biggles. 'Does that mean anything to you?'

'Plenty,' answered Biggles. 'I'd have come from England for less.'

'But what is it? What can that scrap of paper tell you?'

'It tells me,' replied Biggles, 'that at least one of your crooks was a foreigner. He was recently in Monte Carlo. Also, he has the rather unpleasant habit of picking his teeth.'

Brand blinked. 'Are you kidding?'

Biggles shook his head. 'This is no time for fooling, Brand. This scrap of paper contained a sterilized toothpick which was made in Paris. In France, where toothpicking after a meal is a common practice, toothpicks are either to be found on the tables of the big hotels or will be supplied on request. This particular specimen was supplied to a Hotel de Paris, of which there are several in France. But the most celebrated Hotel de Paris is in Monte Carlo, hence the letters MC. Your bandits, Brand, were no local bush-rangers. So much, at least, we have discovered. What's Joe got now? He's just picked something up. The draught we made seems to have uncovered more than tracks.'

Joe, who had been nosing about where the soft sand had been cleared, came back with a button. There was nothing remarkable about it. It appeared to be an ordinary button from the cuff of a man's jacket. The colour was greenish-grey.

'You're doing fine, Joe,' Biggles told him. 'Go ahead and find some more.'

Joe did his best while the others watched; but there was nothing else.

An hour was spent surveying the site of the tragedy. In the middle of the track was a large hole. Around it lay scattered the wreckage of the ill-fated jeep. The footprints to which Brand had referred were still there in a well-trampled area, where presumably the bandits had unloaded the gold.

'I think it's all fairly clear,' said Biggles. 'The plane landed some distance away and unloaded the gunmen. They took up positions in the bushes. When they had done their dirty work the plane came over and landed where we found its tracks. With the gold loaded up it took off. Where it went is anyone's guess. It could be anywhere in the world. Sooner or later, no doubt, it would make for Europe, where there is a ready market for gold – and no questions asked.'

'What are you going to do next?' inquired Brand.

'As there's nothing more we can do here we'll take you home and then start back for England,' answered Biggles.

'We shall refuel at Darwin and perhaps spend the night there. I'm well satisfied with the results of the trip. I'm much obliged to you for your help, Brand.'

Thus it was decided. Biggles took the mine manager and his tracker back to Barula Creek, and stopping there only long enough for a cup of tea, took off again and headed north.

'What did you make of that wheel track?' Biggles asked Ginger as the Wellington droned on over the dreary waste.

'I've no figures on me, but I'd say it was made by a DC3 fitted with a tricycle undercart,' answered Ginger. 'I can check up when we get home.'

'That's what I think,' replied Biggles. 'Which means that the track could have been made by the machine Marcel told us about. Unfortunately, as there must be thousands of DC3s in service, in one part of the world or another, it doesn't help us much in the way of identification. More than one may have been fitted with a tricycle undercarriage. We'll go into that when we get back.'

'Such a machine would be just the job for air pirates,' opined Ginger. 'Surely the one that came here must have refuelled somewhere?'

'We can make inquiries as we go home,' rejoined Biggles. 'Mind you, with nothing much to carry it would have a big endurance range, particularly if it was fitted with spare tanks. We'll ask Darwin if they've any record of such a machine.'

'What about this dud newspaper reporter? Where did he come from? A small machine like a two-seater must have refuelled all along the line, unless it was bought in this country.'

'We'll check up on him, too,' promised Biggles. 'If he was genuine it should be an easy matter to find out the name of the newspaper that financed him.'

The sun was well down when the Wellington reached Darwin, where Biggles had decided to refuel and spend the night in order to start fresh on the long journey home. He had just switched off when an exclamation from Ginger brought his head round. 'What is it?' he inquired.

Ginger pointed to a small machine standing on the tarmac. 'That answers to Brand's description of the newspaper man's plane,' he said tersely. 'That's an Aeronca – American. Look at the colour. I'd call that brownish-green.'

'By Jove! You're right,' returned Biggles. 'This is where we start asking questions.'

They all walked over to the control office, where they were greeted by a flight officer named West, whom they knew because Biggles had shown him his credentials on the way out.

'Any luck?' inquired West, as they drew near.

Biggles pointed to the Aeronca. 'Who does that machine belong to?'

'Len Holmes.'

'Who's he?'

'He runs a little flying-school here, and a fly-yourself service. There he is, just going to pull the Aeronca in.'

'I'd like a word with him. Will you call him over?'

'Sure.' West whistled, and beckoned. Holmes came across, and Biggles was introduced. 'Bigglesworth runs the Air Police in England,' explained West. 'He wants to ask you about that Aeronca of yours.'

'I bought it,' declared Holmes, looking indignant.

Biggles smiled. 'I'm not accusing you of pinching it. Tell me this. Did you by any chance hire out that machine about a month ago to a little dark chap?'

'Newspaper man?'

'That's right.'

'I certainly did,' stated Holmes. 'I'm not likely to forget him. He said he'd only be gone an hour or two, but he was away all day. I thought he was down in the bush, and was just going out to look for him when he rolled up. He said he'd had a spot of engine trouble but had managed to put it right. Sounded a funny sort of tale to me.'

'What was his name?'

'Canton. At least, that was the name on his licence. I had a look at it, you may be sure. If I remember right, it was issued in 1939. He was a chap about thirty-five, I'd say.'

'Was this a Royal Aero Club ticket?'

'Sure it was – a B Licence, too. If he was good enough to fly for hire in England that was good enough for me.'

'Where did he come from? I've a reason for asking these questions.'

'I don't know. He rolled up on a motor bike and said he just wanted to put in a bit of flying time for practice. He seemed to have plenty of money.'

'Did he pay you himself, or did he ask you to send the bill to his paper?'

'He paid me himself, in cash.'

'And he gave you the impression that he was just having a joy-ride on his own account?'

'Yes.'

'At Barula Creek,' said Biggles slowly, 'he led them to believe that he was on a job for his paper.'

Both Holmes and West stared. 'So that's where he went?' burst out Holmes.

Biggles nodded.

'By thunder! No wonder he wanted to make sure his tanks were topped up!'

'Even so, it's hard to see how he could have got to Barula Creek and back,' said Biggles quietly.

Holmes looked nonplussed. 'He couldn't have done it,' he declared. 'His tanks were half-full when he got back. If he went to Barula Creek he must have got some more petrol from somewhere, and there's no pump that I know of in the outback.'

'There's only one way he could have got it,' said Biggles.

'What do you mean by that?'

'The Aeronca wasn't the only machine in the outback that day.'

West clicked his fingers. 'That's it!' he cried. 'Funny you should say that, because it throws light on something that's puzzled me a lot. My guess is the other machine was a DC3.'

'Have you seen one?' asked Biggles sharply.

'I sure have,' declared West. 'A DC3 went over here one day without calling. That's unusual, because practically every machine coming from the north puts in here to refuel. This one went right on. In fact, it seemed to sheer off. It was pretty high, so thinking the pilot might have lost his way, I signalled all stations to be on the lookout for him. I also tried to make contact with the machine, but if he got my signals he didn't answer. As far as I can make out he didn't land anywhere. At least, I've had no record of a landing. I said to myself, well, if he's down, he's down. We can't search the whole blooming continent every time a chap gets off his course.'

'He made no signal?'

'Not a squeak.'

'But if he was lost he'd have asked for his position.'

'You'd think so. Anyway, he didn't call, so it was really no affair of mine.'

'You didn't happen to notice if this kite had a tricycle undercart?'

'No. He was too far off.'

'Hm,' mused Biggles. 'Did you see anything more of this chap Canton?'

West answered. 'No. When he didn't come to my office I tried to find him. He should have signed my book.'

'So you don't know where he went?'

'I haven't the foggiest. He just faded away. I've still got a blank space in my book.' West frowned. 'D'you think he had anything to do with the gold robbery?'

'Could have,' answered Biggles non-committally. 'But say nothing to anyone about that. I'd like you to do this for me. If either of you see or hear anything of this DC3 again, or this fellow Canton, I wish you'd let me know. A cable to Scotland Yard will find me.'

The two men agreed.

'Thanks very much, chaps, for being so helpful,' said Biggles. 'We shall stay the night. In the morning we'll top up and start for home. Meanwhile, mum's the word. So long.' With the others he walked towards the airport exit.

'The pattern of this business begins to take shape,' he resumed, as they walked on. 'Marcel seems to have been on the track, too, with his story about that DC3 that no one owns. As I see it, what happened was this. The bandits came here in a Douglas DC3. This fellow Canton was one of them. They came from the north. They made the usual landfall, Port Darwin, to check their bearings, but they didn't stop. Apparently having plenty of petrol, they landed some distance on, well inside the country. Having parked themselves Canton unloads a motor bike and slips into Darwin to hire a machine. He couldn't get all the way to Barula Creek on a motor bike, for obvious reasons. Having hired the Aeronca, he flew to the mine, where, acting as a newspaper reporter, he got the information he needed. He then flew the Aeronca back to Darwin, refuelling at the Douglas on the way. He probably got petrol from the Douglas going both ways. Anyway, he knew where he could get petrol if he wanted it. He then returned to the Douglas on his motor bike. The big machine then moved nearer to the place decided on for the ambush. It all worked out as planned. After the jeeps had been shot up the Douglas was brought right in to where I landed the Wellington this morning. The gold was loaded up, and away it went. They probably reckoned on their engines smothering their landing-track with sand. No doubt they hoped that no one would associate an aircraft with the job. It was the last thing to occur to Brand, as you may have noticed. When you come to think of it, it was all very simple. It could hardly go wrong. Where these thugs have gone is anyone's guess. They wouldn't be likely to stay in Australia, where they'd find it difficult to sell the gold without questions being asked. They'd move nearer to an easier market – to Europe, no doubt. Well, taking this trip of ours all round, it's been well worth while. We've learned a lot more than I expected. In the morning we'll push along home as fast as we can to see if there are any developments there.'

5

INVESTIGATIONS

A week after the incidents narrated in the foregoing chapter Biggles was home again, somewhat tired after long hours in the air; for, as many people have discovered, there are few vehicles more tiring than an aircraft when there is nothing to relieve the tedium. Admittedly, speed is achieved, but that, unfortunately, is not evident during the process. No reptile appears to move more slowly than an aircraft at a high altitude. And, as Biggles remarked to the others *en route*, as the world was a big place, and an aeroplane a very small object, they were likely to be even more tired before their quest for the air bandits bore fruit.

However, there was plenty to do at Operational Headquarters. To save time Biggles had made a signal to Algy, from Egypt, asking him to check up, through the Air Ministry, on the pilot Canton. This had been done, and Algy's report was waiting. There was nothing much to it, but what there was went some way towards confirming what was already known. Canton had learned to fly before the war. He had flown with the RAF during the early part of the war, but had been discharged on medical grounds as the result of a crash. Later he had made a complete recovery and had qualified for a pilot's B Licence, which permitted him to 'fly for hire'. This had been cancelled in 1949 following a conviction in a civil court for importing watches by air without declaring them to Customs; in simple English, smuggling. For the same reason his name had been erased from the list of members of the Royal Aero Club. After that he had faded out of aviation circles. His present address was unknown.

'Same old story,' observed Biggles, on reading the report. 'Once a crook always a crook. He'll finish where they all end up.'

What was perhaps more important than this, Marcel had been on the phone during Biggles' absence, but on learning from Algy that he was abroad had asked to be notified of his return as he had something to say. Contact was made with him in Paris, and he said he would come over right away.

In the meantime Biggles sent Algy to Scotland Yard with the button found at the scene of the hold-up. His instructions were to see Inspector Gaskin of C Division and get expert opinion on it. Again the report was meagre, although this was only to be expected. The button was of German manufacture. It was plastic of a somewhat unusual type, made by a firm in Hamburg. It was standard in size and shape, and had probably come off the cuff of a sports jacket of greenish material. It would probably be difficult to replace outside Germany.

'Which means,' remarked Biggles, 'that one of the gang either has a button still missing from his cuff, or an odd one. He may not have noticed that the button is missing.'

'Is this the fellow who picks his teeth, do you suppose?' inquired Ginger.

'It could be. But there must have been at least four of them in the aircraft that went to Australia, and it might have come off the jacket of any one of them.'

One other detail appertaining to the case came as an inquiry put through Air Commodore Raymond, to whom Biggles reported his return by telephone. No sale or movement of any quantity of gold, such as would happen if the stolen gold had reached the open market, had been noticed. This meant that the bandits had not yet disposed of their haul; or if they had, it had gone to black-market operators who had so far kept it under cover.

They were discussing the different aspects of the case when Marcel Brissac arrived. He had flown over in his Morane, and breezed in with a cheerful enthusiasm that gave cause to suppose he had important information to impart. This, however, was not so – or so it appeared at first glance. Such news as he had was negative. The gist of it was this.

He had been busy; and this, at any rate, was certainly true, for it transpired that he had flown over most of North Africa, making inquiries at military and civil airports about an unknown DC3. As these had produced no result, he had switched his questions to another track. These now related to possible landing-grounds or flat areas with a water supply available in the region of the Ahaggar Mountains. The question had been put to French pilots of considerable Saharan experience. They were unanimous in their opinion that there was no place in the central Sahara, outside their own scattered refuelling stations such as the notorious *Bidon Cinq*, where white men could live for any length of time, much less maintain an aircraft. In the whole vast area, Marcel had been told, there was only one white settlement, and this was an artificial oasis occupied by members of a religious order who called themselves the White Prophets of Peace. 'Whoever they are they must be mad to live in such a cauldron,' observed Marcel, with a shrug.

'Men who devote themselves to religion usually choose somewhere pleasant to live – and why not?' remarked Biggles. 'Why make an artificial oasis, anyway? Aren't there enough natural ones in the world?'

'*Mais non!* They did not make the oasis,' explained Marcel. '*Attendez.* I will tell you how it comes there. Years ago there is a man, very rich, very gentle, who loves deserts and the creatures that live in them. Why this should be I cannot comprehend. Perhaps he was a little mad. Who can tell? His name is Monsieur Bourdau. Always he goes to the great deserts, to sit and watch.'

'Watch what?' inquired Biggles curiously.

'The beast that is called the ibex. But this man loves the ibex.' Marcel spoke as if he could hardly believe this himself.

Biggles looked incredulous.

'Why a man should love the ibex is a thing not easy to understand,' admitted Marcel, with another shrug. 'But there, men love different things. This one loved the ibex. Why he loved the ibex – '

'Never mind *why* he loved the ibex,' interposed Biggles. 'Let's agree that he did love them. What about it? Go ahead.'

Marcel went on. 'As Monsieur Bourdau grows old he also grows sad, because he sees that the ibex get less each year. They die because the water dries up. He has an idea. He is rich. The ibex shall be saved. To a valley in the mountains he brings engineers with machines that dig deep in the earth for water. The water rises in the pipe. It fills a trough of stone. The ibex find the trough. They drink. Monsieur Bourdau watches this. He may be mad, but he is happy, because the ibex are saved. Where the earth becomes wet he plants grass and little trees. So is born an oasis. It gets bigger. Monsieur Bourdau builds a house there, a big house for himself and his friends, so that they can watch the ibex. It is a sanct...sanct – '

'Sanctuary.'

'*C'est ca.* That is it. Monsieur Bourdau is content. He lives at El Asile – that is what he names the oasis – until he dies.'

'Then what?'

Marcel raised his hands in an expressive gesture. 'That is all. The ibex drink, but there is no one to watch. Then one day a holy man comes to the French government and says someone should be in the desert to see that the water flows so that the ibex may drink. He will go, and with some friends make a religious house for the memory of the good Bourdau. So they go. Everyone is happy.'

'Including the ibex,' murmured Biggles sarcastically. 'Tell me, Marcel. Where did you collect this fantastic story?'

'From the offices of the Administration in Algiers. The story is, without doubt, true.'

Biggles looked interested. 'Do these ibex watchers, these White Prophets, stay out in the desert all the time?'

'But yes.'

'How do you know that?'

'I speak to a pilot of Air France who one day sees smoke, from their kitchen perhaps.'

'Do these men ever come back to civilization?'

'If they do no one sees them.'

'What do they live on?'

'Who cares?'

'They do, I'll warrant. Even holy men have to eat. They'd soon get tired of sharing the grass with the ibex. If my memory is correct the Ahaggar Mountains are the best part of a thousand miles from anywhere, and that's a long walk every time you want a loaf of bread.'

'That is true,' agreed Marcel, as if this aspect had not occurred to him.

'How many of these White Prophets are there?'

'I do not think the number is known, but perhaps several.'

'It seems to be infectious, this ibex watching.'

Marcel looked pained. 'You do not believe this?'

'I can't believe that these fellows are there merely to watch an animal quench its thirst. They could see that at the zoo. Monsieur Bourdau was genuine, no doubt; but an ibex watcher is something that might occur once in a lifetime. Yet here, apparently, we have a party of them, all content to live alone in the middle of a million square miles of sand, for the pleasure of watching a fool animal wet its whiskers. Are all these men Frenchmen?'

'No one seems to know who they are.'

'I'm surprised your Administration hasn't troubled to find out.'

'They would think, as anyone would think, what mischief could men do in such a place?'

'That may be the very reason why they chose to go there,' said Biggles slowly.

'Shall I fly out and speak to them?' suggested Marcel. 'I could ask them if a strange aeroplane sometimes passes that way.'

'No, I don't think I'd do that,' answered Biggles quickly.

'I might annoy the ibex, you think?'

'You might annoy the men who sit there watching them drink.'

For a moment Marcel didn't get it. Then understanding dawned in his eyes. 'You think these persons have another business at El Asile?'

'Their purpose there may be perfectly innocent, but I'm willing to risk a small bet that they are not there just to watch a herd of ibex stick their noses in a trough. I'll tell you what to do, Marcel. First you go to Paris and make discreet inquiries about these White Prophets. Find out if anyone knows anything about them. Then fly out to El

Asile, very high, and take a photograph of the place. From that we may get a clue as to what these naturalists are doing. Fly straight over, so that they will not suspect that your interest is in them. Bring the photograph here, and we'll study it together. It may tell us nothing, but we've got to start our hunting somewhere.'

'*Bon*. That is easy,' declared Marcel reaching for his cap. 'When I have done this I come back.'

'That's the idea,' confirmed Biggles.

With a cheerful wave Marcel departed.

Biggles turned to the others. 'There's no need for us to do nothing while we're waiting for him to come back,' he said. 'Algy, how would you like a few days on the Riviera? You can take Bertie with you for company.'

'What's the drill?'

'The drill is, you take a room at the Hotel de Paris, in Monte Carlo, and keep your eyes open for a fellow in a greenish sports jacket minus a button off his cuff. You can take the button we found with you, to refresh your memory. Watch the restaurant. He's probably eaten there once, and may do so again. There's also a chance that he picks his teeth. That isn't much to go on, I know, but we may as well make the most of what clues we have. You may spot this fellow Canton, who fiddles with a scar on his head. According to the people in Australia he's about thirty-five, thin, dark, with a little black moustache. He's a pilot, so one of you might keep an eye on the nearest airport, at Nice. He may use it. Bertie has all the gen about these things. You can fly down in one of the Austers if you like, so you'll have to land at Nice, anyway.'

'Okay,' agreed Algy. 'We'll have some decent bathing if nothing else. Come on, Bertie.'

'I'll be here if you want to get in touch with me about anything,' Biggles told them, and then turned to Flight Sergeant Smyth, who was standing in the doorway, obviously waiting to speak. 'Yes, Flight Sergeant, what is it?' he inquired crisply.

There was a curious expression on Smyth's face when he answered. 'Well, sir, I really came to speak to you about some more spares, but I couldn't help hearing what you said about a man named Canton.'

'What about him?'

'There was a man of that name hanging about here yesterday. He was a thin, dark fellow, with a bit of a black moustache.'

Biggles started. 'What! What did he want? You must have spoken to him to get his name?'

'I asked him what he wanted. He said he was a reporter from the *Daily Mail*. He'd been detailed to do a story on the Air Police and wanted some information. He showed me his card. That's how I knew his name.'

Biggles stared. 'Well, stiffen the crows!' he breathed. 'Canton – still playing newspaper reporter. What did you tell him?'

'I told him we were under orders not to talk to the Press.'

Biggles looked worried. 'How long was this fellow here?'

'I don't know, sir. I found him wandering about talking to some of the boys, or trying to. I told him to push off. It seems he was asking for you, personally, but was told you didn't see anyone. He said was it right you were just back from Australia?'

Biggles looked at the others in turn. 'Can you beat that for sheer brass face?' he muttered. He turned back to the Flight Sergeant. 'What became of this chap at the finish?'

'He went off.'

'How – was he walking, motoring, flying...?'

'I didn't notice, sir. It didn't seem important.'

'Hm. All right, Flight Sergeant. I'll speak to you about the spares presently. Tell the boys on no account to talk to strangers. If you see any about let me know.'

'Very good, sir.' The Flight Sergeant started to move off.

Biggles called him back. 'Just a minute,' he said, a hint of anxiety in his voice. 'This fellow could have been here some time?'

'Yes, sir. I didn't see him arrive. I was busy on a job in the hangar.'

'I see.' Biggles spoke slowly and thoughtfully. 'In that case it might be a good thing if you made a thorough inspection of any machines that were standing outside. This chap Canton may have got up to some monkey business, apart from asking questions. Start with J-4578. Mr Lacey will be using it presently.'

'Very good, sir.' The Flight Sergeant strode away.

Biggles turned again to the others, who were still standing there. 'This is a fast one I did not expect,' he confessed, and then smiled ruefully. 'While we were looking for the enemy he was right here on our doorstep, playing cat and mouse. If he found out that I'd been to Australia he'd know why. Well, well. We shall have to watch how we go with this gang. As I said before, at least one of them has brains – and uses them.'

'Do you really think they might try to sabotage our machines?' asked Algy.

'I'd put nothing past them,' answered Biggles. 'Murder is nothing to them; witness the way they shot up the gold convoy. Sabotage would be less than nothing if it suited their purpose. And, after all, that might be the easiest way to put us out of business. It was the first thought that came into my head when Smyth said this fellow Canton had been here. But you had better be getting along if you want to make Nice in daylight.'

Algy and Bertie picked up the emergency valises containing their small kit, kept packed for instant use, and departed.

Biggles settled down at his desk.

Ten minutes later the door opened and Algy reappeared. His face was pale. 'Come and take a look at this,' he invited, in a tense voice.

Without a word Biggles followed him to the Auster. Ginger went with them.

'What do you make of that?' asked Algy, pointing. 'We were just going to start up when Smyth spotted it.'

Following the direction indicated, Ginger saw a sort of swelling on the rear exhaust pipe, four of which projected below the engine cowling. Moving nearer, he observed that something had been bound on the pipe with black adhesive tape, so that in the ordinary way it would not have been noticed.

Biggles took out his penknife and opened the small blade. 'Stand well back everyone,' he ordered curtly. Then, slowly and with infinite care, he raised the end of the tape and unwound it. A metal tube came into view. Very, very carefully, in dead silence, he removed it, and with a deep breath, stepped back. 'I don't know what this is,' he said in a hard voice. 'But I can guess. It looks like one of those small gelignite demolition bombs that were issued to Commandos in the war. The heat of the exhaust, when the engine was started, would, I imagine, have been enough to do all that was necessary. There would have been a loud bang. The aircraft would have disintegrated – and we should never have known why. I'll get the experts at the Yard to examine this.' He turned to Flight Sergeant Smyth. 'Make a thorough examination of the other machines,' he ordered. 'Be careful, and do the job properly.' He looked at the others. 'See what I mean about watching our step? The enemy knows we're on the job. He's on the job, too. All right. The machine is probably okay now.'

'I hope you're right, old boy,' said Bertie, with unusual earnestness.

6

A MAN MINUS A BUTTON

Algy stood on the famous terrace at Monte Carlo, in the Principality of Monaco, in the South of France, and regarded the Mediterranean Sea with something like despondency. He and Bertie had been on the celebrated Blue Coast for five days, and as far as results were concerned they might as well have stayed at home. All they had gained was a change of climate, and this, admittedly, was for the better, as the weather could with truth be described as perfect. Contact with Biggles, informing him of failure, had merely brought the laconic reply 'stick to it'.

Algy had, of course, realized from the outset that their chances of success were slim. He knew that Biggles knew that, too, when he had detailed him for the job. To find a man minus a cuff button had seemed a forlorn hope even from a distance; on the spot it seemed a complete waste of time. One man in every six appeared to wear a jacket that could, by stretching the term, be described as green; and the buttons on every one, as far as could be ascertained, were complete.

Bertie had gone to the airport at Nice to have a look round. They had taken it in turns to go. The luck there had been no better than in Monaco.

The day was hot, the sort of day that encouraged thirst, so although he had just had his lunch Algy strolled over to the bar of the Café de Paris, where he could drink an iced lemon squash in the shade. There was only one other customer there. Paying no attention to him, he ordered his drink, took a cigarette from his case, flicked his lighter and lit the cigarette. A voice at his elbow said: *'Merci, monsieur,'* and turning, he saw that his companion was holding an unlighted cigarette. Algy held out the lighter. He still paid no attention – that is, until the man's hand went to his lips, which brought his sleeve into view. Algy's eyes went to the usual row of buttons on the cuff. As he had been looking at cuffs for the past five days this was largely automatic. One, the bottom one, was missing. The two that remained were similar, if not identical, to the one he had in his pocket. Only the jacket was not so much green as grey, which was probably why it had not previously been investigated; for Algy, now that he really looked at his companion, perceived that he had seen him two or three times before, usually going in or coming out of the casino.

To describe Algy's emotions as he returned the lighter to his pocket would not be easy. The dominant one was astonishment, which was so acute as to induce a sensation of unreality. Now that he had practically given up looking for a man minus a cuff button here was one standing beside him drinking a whisky and soda. Could it be possible, he wondered, that this man had recently been to Australia on a criminal enterprise? No, he decided, it could not. The thing was too fantastic. Yet why not? Someone had certainly been to Australia, and it might as well be this man as any other. Anyhow, as he had found precisely what he had travelled to Monte Carlo to find, he might as well see the thing through. Thus whirled Algy's thoughts, as out of the corners of his eyes he had a good look at the man who had lost a button.

That he was not British, or French, had been evident from his accent when he spoke. The jacket, and the grey flannel trousers he wore with it, had a continental cut. Algy decided that he might be German, Austrian, or a Czech. It was not easy to guess in an international resort like Monte Carlo, where in a short walk it is possible to see every nationality on earth. His age he put at about forty. For the rest he was tall, fair, and good-looking in a heavy sort of way.

Algy was trying to think of a reasonable excuse to open a conversation when the man finished his drink and walked away. Following, Algy noticed that he walked with a slight limp. Was this another link with Australia? He recalled that the black trackers had declared that one of the bandits walked with a limp. They had all, it was asserted, worn shoes with crêpe rubber soles. This man wore white buckskin shoes which appeared to have crêpe soles. He walked across the road and boarded the little bus which plies between the Place Casino and the bathing-beach, a trifle more than a mile distant. He took a place in the front. Algy also boarded the bus and found a seat in the rear. In a few minutes the vehicle, full to capacity, proceeded to its destination.

On reaching it the man went to the little office, took a ticket, presented it to the woman in charge of the cabins, and was given in return a costume, a towel, and a key from the board on which the cabin keys hung in numbered rows. Algy did the same thing, and was in consequence given a cabin next in line with the one taken by the man he was following, the numbers being twenty and twenty-one respectively. Actually, he was still not clear as to what he was going to do. He had made no plan. So far his intention was simply to keep the man under observation.

The cabins at Monte Carlo bathing-beach are not the flimsy wooden erections one so often finds at home. They are permanent buildings, like a row of bungalow cottages, the doors placed in pairs with a verandah to each pair. Each is furnished like a bathroom. This Algy discovered when, after his man had entered his cabin, he let himself into his own. He watched, and presently had the satisfaction of seeing the man emerge ready for the water. He watched him lock his door, limp along and hang the key on the board, run down to the sea and strike out for the big raft which is moored about two hundred yards from the beach.

Algy did some quick thinking. Then he moved fast. He, too, got into his costume and took his key to the board. But instead of leaving his key he lifted the key of number twenty. There was no risk in this, because the woman in charge was busy hanging out some towels to dry. With the key in his hand he went back to the cabins. A glance revealed that the man was still swimming towards the raft, which he had nearly reached, and towards which, naturally, he was looking. In a moment Algy had unlocked the door of number twenty, gone in and closed it behind him.

The grey jacket hung on a hook. He explored the pockets. Only the breast pocket yielded anything of interest. There were two letters. One was a bill from a tailor in Hamburg, and the other a receipt from a hotel in Berlin. Each envelope bore the same address, and this gave Algy the information he most needed. He made a note of it. It was Herr Wilhelm Groot, Villa Hirondelle, Eze, Alpes Maritimes, France.

Algy replaced the letters, pulled a button off a cuff for comparison, and after a cautious peep slipped out and locked the door. In a matter of minutes he had replaced the key in its proper place and returned to his own cabin, where he compared the button he had taken with the one in his pocket – the one that had been chiefly responsible for his mission. All doubt was dispelled. They were identical. So far so good. He had found such a man as the one he was looking for, although whether he was *the* one remained to be determined. As Groot was still on the raft, Algy had a quick dip. Refreshed, he dressed, returned his key, and went to the exit to wait.

It was half an hour before the man emerged. The bus was there. He boarded it. So did Algy. Together they alighted at the Café de Paris. Groot sat at an outside table and ordered tea. Algy, at a discreet distance, did the same. From the way Groot kept his eyes on the road, and from time to time glanced at his watch, Algy formed the opinion that he was expecting someone. In this he was right, for presently, when a small, but fast-looking sports car, painted blue, pulled in at the kerb, Groot raised a hand, presumably to indicate his position. The car bore a French registration number. Algy memorized it.

The driver alighted, and as Algy's eyes went over him he felt his pulses quicken. He was a man of about thirty-five, slim, dark, and dapper, with a little black moustache. He wore a navy blue suit. Could it, thought Algy, be Canton, the pseudo-newspaper man? The description fitted. When the fellow joined Groot at his table, and on sitting down took off his hat, the description fitted even better, for his hair was brushed straight back without a parting. When almost at once he began running his fingers through it, Algy felt confident, for the first time, that he had found what he was seeking. If this was coincidence, he pondered, it was a remarkable one. From his actions and the way he spoke the dark man appeared to be apologizing for being late. Groot gave an order to a waiter, who presently brought fresh tea and some sandwiches.

The two men, with their heads together, now carried on an earnest conversation. Algy would have given a lot to know what they were talking about, but to try to find out was, of course, out of the question. The sandwiches finished, Groot beckoned a waiter again and asked for something. The waiter looked round, walked to another table and returned with a small glass receptacle. Groot reached for it, stripped a small object of its tissue-paper wrapping, and began picking his teeth.

Now there was nothing really remarkable about this if what Algy had good reason to suspect was correct. On the contrary, it was to be expected. Yet when it actually happened Algy could hardly believe his eyes. It was like watching a prophecy materialize. Anyway, he was quite sure now that he was outside the realm of coincidence. He, too, called a waiter, and asked for a toothpick. The waiter obliged, and in a moment Algy held in his fingers a replica of the little paper tube which Joe, the black boy, had picked up in the Australian desert.

He was now thinking fast. Having two men to watch, he hoped fervently that he would catch sight of Bertie entering the hotel opposite on his return from Nice; for if the two men separated he would have to decide which to follow. Canton – if the dark man was Canton – had a car. To follow him, as things stood, would be impossible. If both went off in the car he could shadow neither of them. This thought brought him smartly to his feet. A line of taxis stood in the municipal parking place less than fifty yards away. Still watching his men, he went to the leading cab, booked it, sat inside, but told the driver not to move. 'I'm waiting for a friend,' he explained. The driver, content to earn money by doing nothing, resumed his perusal of the evening paper.

Algy watched his men, also the hotel on the other side of the Place Casino, hoping to see Bertie, who should have been back before this. Bertie had still not arrived when, some minutes later, the two men got up and climbed into the blue sports car. As it glided away Algy told his driver to follow it. He gave this order with some anxiety, because it was beginning to get dark, and he was afraid he might lose sight of his quarry.

He was not surprised when the blue car took the Middle Corniche road to the west, for this was the direction of the ancient village of Eze, with its sprinkling of modern luxury villas. Later, the road runs on to Nice. Groot, judging from the letters in his pocket, lived at Eze, or was staying there. And to Eze the two cars proceeded. But just outside the village the leading car turned to the right, up the secondary road that connects the Middle Corniche with the top one, known as the Grand Corniche, some hundreds of feet higher up the hillside.

Algy ordered his driver to drop back a bit, as there was no other traffic on the road and he did not want his men to suspect that they were being followed. After going perhaps half a mile he could hear the leading car honking its horn, just round the next bend. They came upon it suddenly, not realizing that it had stopped. This was only preparatory to entering a private drive. There was a lodge at the entrance. A man was opening heavy iron gates.

'Keep going,' Algy told his driver.

As they passed the gates he saw, in the fading light, on the pillars that supported the gates, the incised words, 'Villa Hirondelle.'

Algy allowed the driver to go a little way, then stopped him and told him to go back to Eze. 'Drive slowly,' he requested. As they passed the drive he saw that the gates were now shut. Of the car there was no sign, but through rows of black cypresses he could see the lights of a house of some size.

It did not take him long to decide on what to do next. In Eze he paid off his car and then walked on to the tearoom and restaurant that occupies a prominent position beside the road. He found a seat at one of the outside tables and ordered a *bock*. To the girl who served him he said: 'It's a long time since I was here. Who lives now at the Villa Hirondelle?'

The girl answered without hesitation, 'Monsieur le Count Heinrich Horndorf.'

'A German, eh?'

The girl shrugged. 'Perhaps. But it is said he is from Austria. We do not see him in the village, which is a pity, for he is very rich.'

'You don't know him?'

'But no, monsieur. Once or twice I see him pass in his automobile. It is *magnifique*.'

'Such a man must have a lot of friends?' prompted Algy.

'Without doubt,' replied the girl. 'Many cars go there.'

'How long has the Count lived at the villa?'

'Nearly two years. The villa was much damaged in the war, but now it has been rebuilt in the grand fashion.'

'*Merci, mam'selle*.' Algy did not know what else to say. He did not like to press his questions too hard. The girl went off to serve another customer.

Algy gave the matter some thought. He was in no particular hurry to get back to Monte Carlo, although naturally he wanted to impart his news to Bertie. There would be no difficulty about getting back, because there were plenty of buses. For that matter he could walk if necessary, for the distance to Monaco was only about four miles. He decided to have another look at the villa, so with this object in view he walked back up the road.

The expedition yielded little in the way of information. All was quiet. There were no longer any lights showing. As he walked slowly past the gates he heard a dog growl. He could not see it, but it was clear that Count Horndorf had taken precautions to discourage trespassers. He walked on a little way, perhaps fifty yards, and then sat down against the hedge to watch. He was there for about half an hour. All that happened was that a small but powerful car of the closed-van type pulled up, honked, the same double honk that the blue car had used, and was allowed to enter. He was too far away to make out details, and he hesitated to go nearer. The car did not return, so after waiting a little longer he made his way back to the main road, where, after a short wait, he was able to pick up a Monte Carlo bus.

He went straight to the hotel, agog to tell Bertie what he had learned. He expected to find him in the restaurant or at the bar. Failing to find him, he went up to his room, but he was not there, either. The hall porter had not seen him. No one had seen him. Disappointed, Algy sat in the vestibule to wait, concluding that Bertie had gone out to look for him.

Time passed. Algy had his dinner. Still he waited. Ten o'clock came, eleven o'clock, midnight. Still there was no sign of Bertie. Algy was puzzled, but not alarmed. He could not imagine what Bertie was doing all this time. Finally, at one o'clock, too tired to keep awake any longer, he went to bed.

At seven o'clock he was knocking on Bertie's door. They had adjoining rooms. There was no answer. He got a chambermaid to open the door with her master key. Bertie was not there. Nor had the bed been slept in. Hardly had he got over the shock of this when another shook him. Bertie's things had gone. Not one article of his kit remained.

Now quite bewildered, Algy made his way to the reception desk to see if there was a message for him. There was no message. In reply to further questions the reception clerk turned up his ledger. 'Your friend, *monsieur*, has departed,' said he. 'He checked out some time during the night. The bill is paid. The room is now vacant.'

Slightly dazed, Algy made his way outside. He walked down the hotel steps like a man in a dream. Crossing the road, he dropped into one of the seats facing the casino and settled down to consider the possible answers to this unexpected conundrum.

7

MORE PROBLEMS

What action to take, or whether he should take any action at all, were the problems now on Algy's mind. He felt he ought to let Biggles know what had happened, yet he hesitated to worry him, perhaps bring him down unnecessarily. There was still a chance that Bertie would turn up. There might be a letter in the post. One thing was certain, Bertie would not have acted as he had without a very good reason, pondered Algy. Bertie was well able to take care of himself. In the end he decided to do nothing in a hurry. He would wait to see if there was a message or a letter.

A letter came in the late afternoon post. He recognized Bertie's handwriting, although the envelope had obviously been addressed in great haste. He tore it open impatiently. Out fell a flimsy slip of paper. There was nothing else. He looked at the slip. It was a receipt issued by the *consigne* (the left-luggage office) at Nice Airport. Nothing had been written on it except a scrawled figure one, indicating that only one piece of luggage had been left. Algy turned the slip over and over, hoping to find a message, but in vain.

This simple yet mysterious document did nothing to ease his mind. Far from satisfying his curiosity, it had the opposite effect. However, he knew now what to do. The answer to his problem, he felt sure, was to be found at the airport, so to it, in a taxi, he sped.

In forty minutes he was there. First he went to the hangar in which the Auster had been parked, to confirm that it had not been taken away. It was still there. Somewhat relieved, he then went to the *consigne* and tendered the receipt.

The woman behind the counter glanced at it, reached to a shelf behind her and produced a large red-and-green silk handkerchief tied by the corners into a small bundle. Algy recognized the handkerchief as Bertie's property. He had often ragged him about it. Picking it up, he took it to the nearest bench and opened it. As he threw back the corners there appeared what he observed to be the contents of Bertie's pockets – a gold cigarette-case bearing his monogram, a notecase with his papers and money, some odd letters, and most remarkable of all, his passport. At these things Algy stared in mute astonishment. He went through the papers twice, at first quickly, then more carefully, looking for a message. There was none. Finally, he gathered the things together and put them in his pockets. He was still without a clue to account for Bertie's disappearance. It was clear, however, that what Bertie had done he had done deliberately. It was equally clear that something important had happened, something of a nature so urgent that it had not been possible to let him know about it. The time had come, he decided, to let Biggles know of this development.

He would have started then and there, for there was just enough time for him to get through in daylight, he reckoned. But he did not feel inclined to leave his things in the hotel bedroom. Moreover, there was the matter of his bill. Wherefore he decided to return to Monaco, clear everything up, and make an early start in the morning.

He considered putting a call through to Biggles, but abandoned the idea on the grounds that the business was too involved for a telephone conversation, which, moreover, might be overheard. On reaching the hotel he made inquiries, but there was no message from Bertie – not that he expected one.

For the rest of the day he wandered about turning the matter over in his mind, without getting an inspiration. All he could think was, Bertie had struck a hot trail, had followed it, and was still following it. But why abandon the very things without which it is impossible to get far in a foreign country – money and identification papers? That Bertie must have had a reason was evident, but what it was defied explanation. Could Bertie, he wondered, have struck the same trail as himself, but from a different angle? There was a chance of it, however improbable it might seem at first glance. If that was so, it might end at the same place as his own, the Villa Hirondelle at Eze. On the spur of the moment he decided to have another look at the place. He might learn something there. There was nowhere else to look, and he had nothing else to do, anyhow. A trip to Eze would help to pass the time, if nothing more profitable. As soon as it was dark, therefore, he boarded a bus and took a ticket to the village. Alighting at the turning, he walked slowly up the road towards the villa, with a vague idea of studying the place at close quarters.

It did not take him long to discover that this was not a practicable proposition. The gates were locked – not that he seriously contemplated entering the grounds as brazenly as that. He sought a more secretive way, but he sought in vain. In short, a reconnaissance lasting about an hour revealed that the entire property was surrounded by one of those vertical wire fences, with spikes turned over alternately at the top, that are practically insurmountable. Presently he was glad that this was so, for returning to the gates he was confronted by two snarling Alsatians – fortunately on the other side. He backed away quickly for fear they would bring out the lodge-keeper. There was, he saw, nothing more he could do, for he had no intention of taking on a pair of savage Alsatians with his bare hands. There was no question at this stage of using lethal weapons against them.

So, reluctantly, he abandoned his project; but as it was a warm moonlight night, and he was not in a hurry, he did not immediately hasten away. He retired to the hedge, rather nearer to the gates than on the previous occasion, and settled down to await events, if any. For a long time nothing happened. The gates were not opened. But at about half-past ten, just as he was thinking of going home, he saw the lights of a car coming up the road. They stopped at the gates, and in the bright moonlight he saw the same vehicle which he had seen before, a small but powerful-looking van, painted dark blue or black – he could not be sure which. It struck him that it had exceptionally heavy tyres, with a deep tread, for a vehicle of its size. It was the sort of car a farmer might use for getting about over rough ground. That was all he saw. The car gave the usual double honk. The gates were opened. The car drove in. The gates were shut and locked. In the direction of the house, through the spire-like cypresses, lights appeared. A faint murmur of conversation reached his ears, together with a succession of scraping noises followed by thuds as if luggage was being unloaded. The sound stopped. The lights went out. Silence returned. Algy got up, walked down to the main road, caught a bus home, and went to bed.

He was up early, and having had some coffee, checked out and called a taxi. He was at the airport before ten o'clock, with his kit, and with the whole day before him in which to get home.

An incident now occurred for which he was entirely unprepared. As he walked round the end of the hangar which housed his machine he saw Canton, or the man he believed to be Canton, chatting to a mechanic. They appeared to be on familiar terms, which again supported his belief that the man was Canton, for only a man connected with aviation would be in the hangar. The two were standing near a Mosquito in the same shed as Algy's Auster, which was standing end on, ready to come out. This last detail was probably responsible to some extent for what happened.

On seeing Canton, Algy had stepped out of sight promptly, not because he had any reason to suppose that the man knew of his connection with the Air Police, but simply because he preferred not to be seen. He could see everything perfectly well from a safe distance, anyway.

The conversation finished, Canton was walking away when he appeared to notice the Auster for the first time. He stopped abruptly, looked hard, and then moved his position to one from which he could read the registration letters. That he had not noticed the machine before was probably due to the position in which it had been parked, thought Algy, who could have kicked himself for an oversight that he now saw might have far-reaching effects. It looked as if Canton had recognized the Auster. After the attempt made to sabotage it the number should have been changed.

Canton said something to the mechanic. What he said, or what the mechanic answered, Algy could not hear. Canton then put a hand in his pocket, took out some money, and handed it to the mechanic, apparently, from the way he went off, with a request that he should purchase something for him. The moment the mechanic was round the corner Canton went quickly to the Auster and looked closely at the rear exhaust.

Algy knew why, and any lingering doubts he may have had about the man's identity were swept away. Canton had recognized the machine as the one he had tried to sabotage on its home airfield at Air Police Headquarters. Now he was wondering how the machine had got to the South of France; why his scheme had failed. Hence his interest in the exhaust. Algy continued to watch. After a swift glance around, Canton went over to a workbench, and selecting a hacksaw strode back to the Auster.

Algy waited for no more. Whatever the consequences might be, he was not prepared to stand by and watch his machine put out of action, for that was obviously Canton's intention. Apart from anything else, he wanted to fly home in it without delay. So, whistling, he stepped forward. Canton, hearing him, stepped back.

Algy nodded. 'Good morning,' he greeted cheerfully.

'Good morning,' replied Canton, recovering swiftly from momentary embarrassment. 'Do you happen to know who this machine belongs to?'

'How would I know?'

'You down here on holiday?'

'Ran down for a spot of sunshine.'

At that moment the mechanic returned and handed to Canton a packet of cigarettes which apparently he had been sent to fetch. That ended the conversation. 'Well, I'll be getting along,' said Canton. 'So long.'

Algy watched the man walk to his blue sports car and drive off. He was thinking fast. That Canton had recognized the machine was certain. Had he recognized him as a member of the Air Police? He thought not. At all events, he had not appeared to associate him with the machine. He perceived he had been lucky to arrive when he did, otherwise he would almost certainly have taken off in a damaged machine. He broke into a perspiration at the thought, for if there is one thing that scares the average pilot it is the possibility of structural failure. For the second time in a few days he had had a narrow escape.

Ten minutes later he was in the air, heading for the Rhone valley, and home.

When he walked into the office he found Biggles and Ginger having tea.

'Hello!' greeted Biggles. 'So you've decided to come home? Where's Bertie?'

'That,' answered Algy, 'is what I'd like to know.'

Biggles' eyes switched to Algy's face. 'What's happened?' he asked shortly.

Algy tossed his kit into a chair and sat down. 'It's a long story.'

'Okay. Let's have it. Take your time. Pour him out a cup of tea, Ginger.'

Algy told his story from beginning to end, omitting nothing, but without any trimmings. Biggles listened without once interrupting. At the finish he said: 'Well done. You've done a good job. Now we're on a trail worth following.'

'But what about Bertie?'

'What about him? It's hard to see how we can do anything at the moment. Nor can I see any reason to panic. He's obviously running fast on a high scent. He'll come back.'

'But what could have made him unload everything he had in his pockets?'

'Obviously he didn't want them on his person.'

'Why not?'

'Again, fairly obviously, he wanted to get rid of all signs of his identity.'

'Why didn't he come and speak to me when he collected his kit at the hotel?'

'We don't know that he did collect his kit. That could have been done by someone else. If Bertie did it, then he wasn't alone, or he would have spoken to you. But not so many questions. Give me a minute to think about this.'

Biggles, a cigarette smouldering between his fingers, devoted himself to serious thought for a good ten minutes. Then he went on.

'What I think happened was this. It's only surmise, of course. At Nice Airport Bertie struck the same trail as you did, in a different place. You saw Canton at Monte Carlo. He may have seen him at Nice. After all, you saw him at Nice yourself, later on. He decided to follow the fellow. There was no time to get in touch with you. It looks to me as if he might have spoken to the man, and then went off with him, in which case he certainly wouldn't want in his pockets documents connecting him with the police. Apparently he didn't want his name to be known, either, or he wouldn't have parted with his passport. He put his things in the cloakroom. In sending the receipt to you he served two purposes. He safeguarded them, knowing that you would collect them, and at the same time let you know that he was on the trail of something and was pushed for time. If Canton is living at the Villa Hirondelle, and it seems that he is, Bertie may have gone there with him. Wherever he went he was on something hot, we can be sure of that, or he would have got in touch with you. I don't think we can leave him down there on his own. He may still try to contact you at the hotel when he gets an opportunity. Apart from that, I feel we ought to keep an eye on the Villa Hirondelle. There's a hook-up between that place and Nice Airport. At any rate, Canton is evidently using the aerodrome.'

'What's the drill, then?' inquired Algy.

'You'd better go back.' Biggles smiled lugubriously. 'Take a different machine this time, or something unpleasant may happen. You don't want to take off with one of Canton's squibs on board. Hire a car to drive yourself when you get there. You'll need to be mobile to watch both the villa and the airport.'

'What are you going to do?'

'I shall have to stay here. I'm still waiting to hear from Marcel. He's gone to get a photo of El Asile, you remember? I expected him back before this.'

'I think I can see him coming now,' put in Ginger, who was standing by the window.

Five minutes later Marcel burst into the room. His customary smile was absent. His manner was peculiar, to say the least of it, as he turned accusing eyes on Biggles. 'What happens?' he demanded.

Biggles stared. 'I'm waiting for you to tell me.'

'Why do you shoot at me?'

Biggles sat back. 'Just a minute. What are you talking about, Marcel? Why should I shoot at you?'

'That is what I ask,' retorted Marcel stiffly.

'I have not been in the air since I last saw you,' stated Biggles. 'Just keep calm and tell me what this is all about.'

'Your friend, Bertie. This one who wears a glass in his eye. He shoots at me. Do you tell him to do this? Is it a joke?'

'Were you flying at the time?'

'Yes.'

'And was Bertie flying, too?'

'Of course.'

'What machine was he flying?'

'A Hurricane.'

'Really! And where did this happen?'

'Over the Ahaggar.'

'Nonsense!' broke in Algy. 'Bertie's in the South of France.'

'But I tell you – '

Biggles raised a restraining hand. 'Just a minute everybody. Sit down, Marcel. Take it quietly. Tell us what happened.'

Marcel explained. 'Yesterday I am flying over the Ahaggar to make a photo of El Asile. I am high, like you say, at three thousand metres. I am alone in a world of mountains and sand. The heat is savage. It is terrifying, but I go on. I see the valley. There are houses. I fly over, making my photographs. Good, I tell myself, now I can go home from this awful place. I pour the sauce.* Then comes a shock. I hear guns. I see bullets fly. Someone is shooting at me. *Mon Dieu!* Am I insane? Can this be possible? Has the heat made me mad? I look. *Voila!* Behind me there is a Hurricane. The pilot is shooting at me. I fly for my life, for I have no guns to shoot back. I am a fool to take off my guns. Bullets pass me to the right, to the left. He is a bad shooter, this man behind me, or I am dead. He cannot hit me. I turn. I make the volplane. All the time he is shooting. Then, suddenly, he is sitting beside me, very close. I look. Who do I see? Now I know I am mad, for it is this man you call Bertie. He makes faces at me, grimaces the most terrible. Also he makes signs with his hands.'

'Ridiculous,' muttered Algy.

Marcel flung his portfolio on the floor with some force. 'Am I blind?' he cried hotly. 'What I say is true. I know this one with the eyeglass. How can there be a mistake? What other man wears an eyeglass when he flies?'

'Let me tell you something,' put in Ginger seriously. 'If Bertie was flying that Hurricane, and wanted to shoot you down, you wouldn't be here now. What he shoots at he hits.'

'And me, so do I,' declared Marcel. 'Tomorrow I put back my guns. When a person shoots at me I shoot back.'

'Keep calm, everyone,' requested Biggles. He looked at Algy. 'Bertie disappeared on Tuesday. Marcel was shot at yesterday. However silly it seems, it was at least possible for

* French flying slang, meaning to fly on full throttle.

Bertie to have got to El Asile in the time – by flying, of course. We must grant Marcel that. Let us assume that the pilot was Bertie. He shot at Marcel, and missed. Missed a sitter. That isn't like Bertie. There's only one answer to that. Bertie wasn't really trying to hit him.'

Marcel flung out his arms. 'But why does he shoot at me? Why does he make faces?'

'I'd say because he was ordered to do it, and daren't refuse. Somebody may have been watching him from the ground. Maybe that's what he was trying to tell you when he was making faces.'

Algy shook his head. 'This all sounds crazy to me. I still say Bertie is in the South of France. Had he been in that Hurricane he would have been his own master, and there would have been nothing to stop him flying home.'

'That,' answered Biggles succinctly, 'would depend on how much petrol he had in his tank. Maybe he didn't want to fly home. The nearest French post where he could get more petrol would be Insalah.'

'That is where I start from,' said Marcel.

'How far is that from El Asile?'

'Five hundred kilometres, at least.'

'Call it three hundred miles. Let us for the sake of argument say it was Bertie in the Hurricane. He must have taken off from somewhere handy. Where else is there but El Asile? If he started from there the people who are running the place would probably see to it that he hadn't enough petrol to get away. He would be given just enough for the job he had to do, which was to shoot down Marcel's Morane.'

Marcel, having relieved himself of his complaint, came back to normal. 'Two French machines have disappeared in the region of the Ahaggar. That is what they tell me at Insalah. It is thought they are lost in the mountains, but now I see perhaps they were shot down.'

'It's a possibility, in view of what you've just told us,' agreed Biggles. 'This whole business seems to be getting into a bit of a tangle,' he went on. 'That was only to be expected, I suppose, since we are now jumping about three continents.' He looked at Algy. 'If Bertie really is in North Africa – although I'm not ready to admit that yet – there isn't much point in looking for him in the South of France. All the same, I still think it would be a good thing if you ran down and had another look at this villa. Something seems to be going on there. Again, no matter where he is now, there's a chance that Bertie may show up in Monte Carlo, in which case he would be looking for you. There may be a hook-up between North Africa and the South of France. Anyway, go back in the morning.'

Biggles turned again to Marcel. 'What about the photos you took at El Asile? Were they any good, and if so, have you brought them with you?'

'But of course. I stopped to have them developed. They show nothing for excitement.' Marcel produced the photos and put them on the table.

'Beautiful photos, anyhow,' observed Biggles, picking up the magnifying glass and studying the pictures while the others looked over his shoulders.

Ginger found himself looking at what is probably the most sterile group of mountains in the world. It was a scene of utter desolation. He remembered that even Arabs born to the desert called it the Land of Fear. He could well understand why. Only in one place was there any relief from the chaos of crumbling peaks which the action of wind and sun was gradually reducing to sand. In the flat bottom of a valley there appeared to be a certain amount of vegetation. At one end of this stood some rambling buildings of which details could not be seen, but which were presumably the headquarters of the White Prophets.

At one place in the valley the print seemed to be blurred, or fogged. He remarked on it to Biggles.

'What you're looking at is dust,' said Biggles. 'I'd say that's the dust raised by the Hurricane as it took off. I can think of nothing else that could have caused it. The machine doesn't come into the picture because it was already out of the field of view. The dust had not time to settle. Well, the photos don't tell us much, but they tell us what we wanted to know. Even if these lonely ibex watchers don't go in for aviation themselves, they know someone who does. An armed Hurricane guards their valley, and that isn't to protect a few ibex. There's something going on at El Asile, and we'll find out what it is. There's no desperate hurry about it. Marcel's appearance may have alarmed them. Of course, this is really a matter for France, but we'd better work together. There's nothing much you can do here, Marcel, so I think you might as well go back to North Africa and stand by in case it is decided to do something about El Asile. By hanging about you might spot the DC3. Algy can go back to the South of France and keep an eye on the villa.'

'Why not ask the French police to raid it?' suggested Algy.

Biggles shook his head. 'We can't afford to risk going off at half-cock. We need more information before we show our hand. That's all for now. I'm going to the Yard to have a word about this with the Air Commodore. It's time he knew how things stand.'

8

BERTIE TAKES A JOB

Biggles' broad summing-up of the situation in the matter of Bertie's disappearance was not far wrong. This is what happened.

Bertie had taken his turn at watching the airport at Nice with no more enthusiasm than had Algy in Monte Carlo. Like Algy, he found the business of watching cuffs for a missing button more than somewhat monotonous. The chances of seeing Canton at Nice seemed very small indeed, with the result that when he did see him his sensations were similar to those of Algy when he found the man with the missing button.

Before that happened there was little Bertie could do except loaf about watching the arrivals and departures of planes and their passengers. He gossiped with the aerodrome staff. If they wondered why he spent so much time hanging about the airfield they said nothing of it. He was not the only spectator, although it must be admitted that most of those who found entertainment at the airfield were boys. Bertie did, in fact, watch the machines coming in and going out because he had nothing else to do, and after all, he had a certain professional interest in them. It was in doing this that he first caught sight of Canton, although he did not know it at the time.

Sitting on a chock on the shady side of the hangar in which his machine was parked, for the day was blistering hot, his attention was attracted to a Mosquito, painted a light shade of blue, coming in to land. He noted that it carried French civil registration marks, and wondered what it was doing there. This interest was purely technical, even after the machine had landed, and was taxying towards him with the obvious intention of using the hangar. The machine stopped when the ignition was cut. The pilot stepped out, and Bertie moved forward for a closer view, his interest still being more in the machine than in the man. Indeed, it was not until the pilot spoke that he really looked at him.

'Pretty to look at, isn't she?' said the pilot, apparently gratified by Bertie's interest, as he pulled off his flying kit and threw it into the cockpit he had just vacated. 'She looks nicer in blue, than in her drab wartime paint. You are British, aren't you?' he added, as if to explain why he had used that language.

'British? Rather. Too true,' asserted Bertie, looking at the speaker.

He saw a slim dark man of about thirty-five, with a small black moustache, smartly dressed – perhaps a little too smartly dressed – in a blue serge suit. For a moment Bertie saw no more than that. It was not until the man ran his fingers through his hair, which was brushed straight back without a parting, that his memory came into play. Even then it did no more than remind him of the description of the pilot Canton, the man he was actually looking for but did not expect to see. He looked again at the man, who, evidently flattered by Bertie's prolonged interest, mentioned that the colour scheme was his own idea.

Bertie's brain was rather slow getting into its stride. So bored had he become with the seemingly hopeless nature of his mission that he hardly thought of success. With a mild shock, he now remembered that Biggles had sent him to the South of France to keep an eye open for just such a man who now stood beside him. Watch Nice Airport, Biggles had said. It's the nearest landing place to Monte Carlo, so there's a chance that Canton may use it.

Pulling himself together, Bertie took a more lively interest in the proceedings. He endorsed the pilot's views with professional knowledge and enthusiasm.

'Are you a pilot by any chance?' asked his companion.

'Rather. Did the war in the jolly old RAF, on Spits,' answered Bertie warmly.

'So did I,' was the reply.

'Jolly good fun – what?' murmured Bertie. 'Peacetime aviating must be pretty binding after the skylarks we had then – if you see what I mean?'

'How right you are. You're not in the service now, by any chance?'

'No. No jolly fear. Too tame. Too bally tame altogether. No use to me – no use at all.'

'Do you get any flying?'

Bertie smiled sadly. 'Can't afford it, laddie.'

'Tough luck. I must give you a flip sometime. I'm often here. My name, by the way, is Canton.'

'Mine's – Smith. Tommy Smith. Good old English name – what?' Bertie had nearly said Lissie. But his brain was now working smoothly, and it struck him, now he was sure of his man, that it might be unwise to give his real name.

Canton threw him a queer look. 'Smith, eh? That's British right enough. Convenient name, too, sometimes.'

Bertie appeared to overlook the implication. He polished his eyeglass briskly while he tried to think of something else to say.

Canton helped him out. 'Are you down here on business or pleasure?'

'Well, neither – if you get my meaning.'

'What are you doing, then?'

'Nothing, old boy. Absolutely nothing.'

'What do you mean by that?'

'Well, you see, being a bit short of cash, I made a raid on the casino in the hopes of filling the old pocket-book.'

'And lost what you had?'

'You know the answers,' said Bertie sadly. 'Matter of fact, I was hanging around here hoping to see someone I know, to get a lift home.'

'Don't say you were crazy enough to come down here without taking a return ticket?'

' 'Fraid I was,' sighed Bertie. 'You're not going to England by any chance?'

'No. Not just now, anyway,' answered Canton, who, judging from his tone of voice, was also doing some fast thinking.

'You – er – wouldn't like to lend me a bob or two, to see me through?' suggested Bertie tentatively.

'Are you broke?'

'Absolutely.'

'You weren't thinking of looking for a job, by any chance?'

'What sort of job? Hard work doesn't agree with me.'

Canton smiled. 'Nor me. I was thinking of flying.'

'Doing what? Flying some silly old josser from one place to another? Not me. That isn't in my line. I like excitement in nice big doses.'

'Maybe I could provide that, too,' said Canton, half jokingly.

'Now you're talking,' declared Bertie.

'Ever fly a Hurricane?'

'Many a time, laddie – many a time. Have you got one you want taking somewhere?'

'I know someone who has. There would be risks, of course.'

'How can you have fun without risks?' inquired Bertie.

'And having started you'd have to go on, whether you liked it or not.'

'Why should I want to stop?'

'The job isn't all lollipops. It might turn out to be something different from what you thought.'

'Then let's have a look at it. I shall jolly soon know.'

'It would mean starting right away.'

'That's how I like things. No messing about. What happened to the chap who was doing the job?'

'He had an accident,' said Canton grimly.

'And what about the rate of pay – if you see what I mean? I hate to raise the question, laddie, but I should have to eat sometimes.'

Canton hesitated. 'As a matter of fact, the final decision in this appointment doesn't rest with me. I work for the same man as you would, if you got the job. But why are we standing here? Let's go to the buffet and have a drink.'

'I say, that's jolly decent of you,' asserted Bertie. 'My tonsils are aching for a bath, positively clamouring for something wet.'

They went to the buffet. Nothing was said on the way. Canton appeared to be thinking. He ordered drinks. 'Look, Smith,' he said, as if he had reached a decision. 'You wait here while I go and have a word with my boss on the phone. I'll only be a couple of minutes.'

'Nothing would move me,' declared Bertie.

He watched Canton go. His brain had not been idle, either. As soon as the man was out of sight he emptied his pockets into his handkerchief, went to the *consigne* and put the bundle on the counter. The woman in charge gave him a receipt. He asked for an envelope. The woman brought one. Into it he put the receipt. He addressed it quickly, to Algy at the hotel, and giving it to the woman with what small change he had left in his pockets asked her to post it. He would have written a note, but there was no time for that. Canton might be back at any moment. As it was, he had only just got back to the bar when Canton reappeared.

'Okay,' said Canton briskly. 'You're to come with me – that's if you're still serious about the job. The boss wants a word with you. I take it you've got your flying licence on you?'

'No, I haven't,' said Bertie.

'He'll want proof that you can fly.'

'I'll soon give him that.'

'How?'

'Should I be such a clueless clot as to get into an aircraft and try to get it off the ground if I couldn't fly?'

'True enough,' conceded Canton.

'I hate to mention it,' said Bertie casually, 'but I haven't any papers on me of any sort.'

'Where's your passport?'

'Some swipe pinched it out of my pocket, with the rest of my things, while I was having a bathe.'

Canton frowned, and for a moment looked disconcerted. 'That's awkward,' he muttered. 'You seem to be in a nice mess one way and another.'

Bertie admitted freely that he was.

'All right. Drink up and let's go,' said Canton. 'I've a car outside.'

Having finished the drinks, he led the way to a blue sports car and drove off in the direction of Nice. Without stopping in the city he took the Middle Corniche road towards Monaco. Before reaching the Principality, however, at Eze he turned sharply to the left, and presently, honking his horn, stopped at the gates of a private drive lined with cypresses. While the gates were being opened Bertie read, on the pillars which supported them, the name 'Villa Hirondelle.'

For a little while Canton left him sitting in the car outside the front door. Then he returned, and two or three minutes later Bertie was being ushered into the presence of the man who, judging from his bearing, and the quality of the appointments of the room, was the boss.

Even before the man spoke Bertie was aware of a commanding personality. Men who are in a position of power, and are conscious of it, exude something. This man did. He looked at Bertie with steady, purposeful grey eyes, as a boy might look at a captured beetle. Bertie, on his part, saw a tall, heavily built, broad-shouldered man of about sixty years of age who carried his corpulence with the dignity of those years. His face was square, and his features so ruggedly prominent that they might have been hacked out of wood. Little bags under the eyes, and jaw muscles beginning to sag, suggested a life of self-indulgence, or at any rate, a lack of physical exercise. He was immaculately dressed in a dark suit. The general impression Bertie formed was, here was a man who, in any walk of life, would have to be reckoned with. There was no clue as to his nationality. No name was mentioned. At the introduction Canton had simply referred to him as The Count.

The Count, who was standing, invited Bertie, with a wave of the cigar he was smoking, to be seated. He himself continued to stand. Bertie knew why, for this is a minor stratagem often practised. A standing man looks down on one seated, and so tends to dominate the situation, even if all other things are equal.

The Count opened the conversation. 'I understand you are a pilot, out of work, looking for a job?' He spoke in a voice in proportion to his size, with a pronounced, though not unpleasant accent. It was the voice of an educated man.

Bertie agreed.

'You have no papers on you?'

'No.'

'No money?'

'No.'

'Where are you living?'

'The Hotel de Paris, Monte Carlo.'

'How can you stay there without money?'

'I haven't paid my bill.'

'Are your things there?'

'What few I brought with me. I didn't expect to stay long. I came to have a fling in the casino. I knew it wouldn't be long before my luck settled things one way or the other.'

'Have you ever been in trouble with the police?'

Bertie hesitated.

'Well – er – not yet,' stammered Bertie.

'What exactly do you mean by that?'

'Well – er – you see, the money I brought down to gamble with wasn't entirely my own.'

'So!' A ghost of a smile appeared for an instant on the Count's face.

'Are you a good pilot?'

'I survived the war.'

'Good at navigation?'

'I can usually find my way.'

'You have flown a Hurricane, I understand?'

'Yes.'

'In combat?'

'Yes.'

'And you'd be prepared to do that again?'

'Who am I expected to fight? I've heard nothing about a war anywhere.'

'You may not have to fight anybody. I employ a Hurricane merely as a precautionary measure to protect certain interests I have in a rather out-of-the-way place I have in Africa. Are you prepared to go there?'

'I'll go anywhere and do anything if the pay packet makes it worthwhile.'

'Have you ever flown big planes?'

'Yes – I've flown all types.'

'Good. I asked because when we know you better, your work, and your range of operations, might be extended.'

'That suits me.'

'In the matter of money you will have no cause to complain,' said the Count quietly. 'Here's something to go on with.' He opened a drawer of his desk and took out a wad of French notes. All were brand new, Bertie noticed.

'You understand that once you have taken my money you are in my employment?' went on the Count.

'Naturally.'

'I dislike using threats, but I must warn you that my interests are widespread. Should you ever work against them it would be known to me at once, in which case it would be a serious matter for you.'

'That's fair enough,' agreed Bertie.

'Are you prepared to go to Africa forthwith? One of my machines will be going very soon.'

Bertie looked surprised. 'Why...yes. But what about my things at the hotel?'

'You needn't trouble about those. I will arrange all that. Canton is going to Africa. You will go with him. You may find the climate rather trying, but that is what I pay well for – among other things. You may not have to stay there long. I have other work for pilots besides protective patrols.'

'I think I should be told what I'm supposed to do,' said Bertie.

'That is a fair question. I have reason to suppose that someone is taking an interest in my property in Africa.'

The Count's calculating grey eyes found Bertie's, and held them. 'It has been reported to me that a member of the French Police has been making inquiries about my business. We do not like the police – but you will have gathered that. Your work will be quite simple. The machine you will fly is fitted with guns. You will discourage visitors by air in the most effective way possible. No one will see what happens.'

'I understand,' said Bertie. Then he smiled. 'There shouldn't be any difficulty about that.'

'I hoped you would see it in that way,' replied the Count seriously. 'Very well. For the time being you will consider yourself on probation. Promotion will depend on your willingness and efficiency. That's all. Don't leave the house in case I need you. Canton will show you the quarters here which I have put at the disposal of my pilots. I think you will find them comfortable.' The Count waved a hand to show that the interview was over.

Outside the door, Canton looked at Bertie and smiled. 'You're okay,' he said. 'Now you're in it's money for jam.'

'You're going to fly me out to Africa from here?'

'From Nice.'

'In the Mosquito?'

'Yes. Don't worry though. Without a war load she's equipped to carry enough petrol to take her to Cape Town, if necessary. Come and have a drink. The Count lays everything on in a big way.'

Wondering if he had been wise to commit himself so definitely, Bertie followed his new colleague to a lounge, where, as Canton had boasted, everything in the way of luxury had been laid on.

9

ALGY LEARNS THE ANSWERS

Algy returned to the South of France with a commission nearly as vague as the previous one. He had found the man minus a button; now he was to watch the house where he lived, or at any rate where he visited – the Villa Hirondelle. Aside from that, he entertained a slight hope that he might see Bertie, for in spite of Marcel's convictions he still found it hard to believe that Bertie could so quickly have been switched to the Sahara. Still, he reasoned, if he had gone there he might come back just as quickly.

He flew to Nice Airport, where he left his machine, a brand new Auster which had just been allocated to the Police Service. In Nice he hired a car, a fast Renault, to drive himself. In it he went on to Eze, where, posing as a tourist, he found accommodation in the Golf Hotel. After filling up with petrol he parked the car in the extensive *Place*, and as the day was drawing to a close he had some food and prepared to keep his objective, the Villa Hirondelle, under observation.

The difficulties confronting him were obvious, and, as he strolled up the road, brought a frown to his forehead. With the Alsatians on the prowl he did not feel inclined to break into the grounds, even if he found a way. He did not see how he could watch the gates in daylight without being remarked by the lodge-keeper; that is, if he remained close enough to serve any useful purpose. By watching after dark he would dare to go nearer; but then his ally, darkness, would make it difficult for him to see anything definite, such as the faces of the people who were using the villa. Everyone came, and went, by car, as was only to be expected considering the position of the house. The local tradespeople, making their deliveries, did not get past the gates, he had observed. They simply rang a bell and handed their parcels to the lodge-keeper. Not much was to be learned by posing as a tradesman, therefore; not that he seriously considered it, because while he spoke French reasonably well, his accent would give him away. He had given some thought to the black van. What did it bring? Obviously, it brought something, or took something away. Where did it come from? When, and where, did it go after it had served its purpose? This was about the only definite factor that he had to work on, and he resolved to follow it at the first opportunity.

The opportunity came that night. He took up a position in the hedge as near to the gates as he dare risk, and there he sat, without anyone coming or leaving, until nearly ten o'clock, when, hungry and thoroughly browned off, he made his way back to the hotel for something to eat. The dinner hour being long past, all he could get was some coffee and a plate of cold ham, which, with crisp French rolls and butter, suited him well enough. It was a fine night, warm and still, so he had the food served on one of the small iron tables outside, a position from which he could watch the road. He did not seriously expect to see anything.

It is at such times, of course, that something happens. He had barely finished his meal, when from the direction of the villa came a vehicle that he recognized at once. It was the small black van. In a moment he was on his feet, hurrying to his car, which stood near at hand. As it turned out, this haste was unnecessary, as the van pulled up at the petrol-pump for fuel. Algy sat in his car, with the engine running, waiting for the van to move off, thankful that here at last there was something he could do. Had he known what lay ahead, his satisfaction would have been somewhat damped.

He was not surprised when the van took the road for Nice. He supposed, without any particular reason, that it was going to the airport. It did not. Leaving the airfield on the left, it carried straight on. It might, thought Algy, be going to Antibes, or possibly Cannes. It passed through these towns without stopping, still travelling fast, as if it still had some way to go.

Algy began to wonder where the chase was going to end. However, having started, he settled down to follow the van however far it might be going.

His wonder mounted as the van drove on, and on. At Frejus they left the sea, but still headed westwards. All Algy knew of the country now was what he could remember from maps. Through villages the van swept on, to Brignoles, and on again towards Aix. Aix reached, still the car did not stop.

Algy began to get concerned about his petrol. Fortunately he had started with a full tank, but he had not been prepared for a run like this. The van must, he decided, be going to Marseilles, or to its big airport some way beyond, at Marignane. They had been on the road four hours, and he was beginning to feel the strain, when the van, instead of turning south to Marseilles, held on almost due west. Algy gave it up. Guessing was obviously futile. He looked at his watch, and the petrol gauge, more often. The thought that the van might outlast him with its fuel supply made him sick with mortification. He knew the country a little better now, or the general layout of it, because he had often used the airport at Marignane. He was driving mechanically, when at four o'clock in the morning the van gave the first sign that it was nearing its destination. It steadied its pace and presently took a narrow side turning to the left. For some time cultivation had been getting sparse, with fewer trees, except for long straight rows of cypresses that had been planted for protection against the *mistral*, the hot wind that in summer blows from the south. On all sides now, in the moonlight, rolled flat, open country, given over to flocks of sheep that somehow managed to exist on a little dry grass.

Algy switched off his lights, which the driver of the van, if he looked back, might regard with suspicion. They were not really necessary, anyway. Soon afterwards the van dowsed its lights, too, but Algy could still see it, a black spot in a world of loneliness. He knew now where they were, for there was only one place in Europe like it. He had seen it often from the air. They had reached the Plaine de la Crau, a vast, stony plain, eighty square miles as flat as a cricket pitch carpeted with nothing but pebbles of all sizes. In the centre of it nothing grows. It is just a stony, sterile wilderness in the most literal sense.

The track, which had for some time been getting worse, gave out altogether at the ruins of what had once been a cottage. A line of ragged, wind-bent cypresses and a heap of grey stones in some parched grass were all that remained. Beyond that there was only stones, nothing but stones. Algy understood now the reason for the extra wide tyres on the van. He tried to go on, but had to give up when his wheels sank in the pebbles. Actually, he could make a little slow progress in first gear, but with the water in his radiator already boiling, he dare not risk going on. Moreover, on the open plain the driver of the van would only have to look round to see him. Stiff and weary, he put the car between the ruins of the cottage and the cypresses, and considered what next to do.

In the clear moonlight he could still just make out the van, perhaps half a mile ahead; and as he watched it he saw a light show for a moment a little way beyond it. Was it, he wondered, a signal? Had the van at last reached its destination? He decided to find out. He could no longer see the van, but he began walking quickly in the direction it had taken. He hated to think how far he might have to go, but was reluctant to admit defeat in the last lap, as he felt sure this must be.

He was right. He had walked less than a mile when a building, or some buildings, became silhouetted ahead against the sky. At first he could not make out what these were. They seemed big. Striding on, he discovered why. The buildings were the skeletons of a line of hangars, put up presumably during the war and now abandoned. He found nothing surprising in this, for if ever an area of ground was a ready-made airfield – apart from the surface – this was surely it. When, soon afterwards, he struck a concrete runway, his opinion was confirmed. He recalled what Biggles had said about the world being littered with abandoned airstrips. Gazing ahead as he walked on he watched the buildings harden in outline. The remains of the airmen's quarters, or administrative buildings, were still there too, he noted. There was no cover of any sort, so he could only hope that he would not meet the van coming back. Drawing near, he saw it standing outside a corrugated-iron bungalow that appeared to be in better repair than the rest.

He hurried on, his weariness falling off him like a garment now that the solution of the mystery – as he had reason to hope – was at hand. Making as little noise as possible on the pebbles, he advanced upon the bungalow, which he could now see was occupied, because although the windows were blacked-out with some flimsy black material, any slight movement of air caused the material to move, showing chinks of light. This told him, too, that the windows were wide open, as they naturally would be after the heat of the day. At the finish he could hear a murmur of voices. Listening, he made out that the language used was German.

Just as he got right up to the building a buzzer zipped a signal. It brought the conversation to an end, except that someone said: 'Good. Here he is, on time.' The voice seemed strangely familiar. An instant later the blind moved slightly, but enough for Algy to get a glimpse of the interior of the room. There were two men there. They were turning towards the door. One was Groot. The other was Biggles' arch enemy, Erich von Stalhein.

Realizing that the men were coming out, Algy sank into the inky shadow of the building – for the moon was now low on the other side – and lay flat. He crept as near to the corrugated iron as possible, pulled his hat down over his eyes, and turned up his collar to show as little of his face as possible. His nerves were tingling from the shock of his discovery. True, Biggles had remarked, to illustrate an argument, that von Stalhein was just the sort of man to be mixed up in the racket he had visualized; but no one had been farther from Algy's thoughts at that moment. The presence of Groot did not surprise him. Apparently he was the driver of the van.

Algy had little time to ponder this startling development. Von Stalhein, now outside, gave a hail, and then rapped out an order. Four men in mechanics' overalls appeared from somewhere, from one of the hangars or adjacent buildings, and stood in attitudes of expectancy. A sound overhead told Algy what they were expecting, and explained the signal. An aircraft was approaching. He could not see it, but from the volume of noise it made he knew that it was gliding. The Plaine de la Crau, or the low-lying marshes of the Camargue that adjoined it, he thought swiftly, would be an ideal place for an aircraft to cross the coast unobserved. Nowhere along the whole North Mediterranean coastline was there a region so lonely, so devoid of human habitation, as this.

Von Stalhein and Groot stood outside the bungalow, talking in low tones, while they waited. Then von Stalhein gave another order. Somewhere a switch clicked, and a widely spaced line of lights, five in all, set in the ground, marked out the concrete runway. Almost noiselessly a big aircraft took shape over it. The pilot made a perfect landing. A touch of throttle was all that was necessary to send it on to the bungalow.

Algy stared at it, but not with surprise. He had a pretty good idea of what the machine would turn out to be. And he was not mistaken. It was a Douglas DC3 – with a tricycle undercarriage. There, not twenty yards away, stood Marcel's mystery plane, resting on its three wheels, its tail raised in level flying position. The landing lights were switched off. The pilot and a passenger got out and walked to the two men who were waiting. Algy recognized one of them. It was Canton. The other, a short, heavily built man, he had never seen before. He noticed that they made little noise on the pebbles as they walked. The reason, he guessed, was because they were shod with crêpe rubber. The machine, Algy supposed, was the one that had made the raid in Australia. If not, it was one exactly like it. The mechanics, obviously the ground crew, closed in on the machine.

'Everything all right?' asked Canton, yawning as if he was tired. He spoke in English.

'Yes. Have you brought the stuff?' asked von Stalhein.

'Sure.'

'Then let's get it out so that Groot can get away before daylight. Groot is to take the machine back.'

'That suits me,' muttered Canton. 'I've seen all I want of it for tonight.'

The ground crew unloaded the 'stuff'. There was not much of it. Five small but obviously heavy sacks were dragged out of the Douglas' cabin and dumped into the van. The contents of the bags, from the dull noise they made in this operation, might have been sand or corn.

'It would have saved a lot of trouble if the old man had brought the lot over in one go instead of in driblets, just to suit that bunch of Roumanian bullion-mongers,' grumbled Canton. 'Still, I suppose he had a reason for it.'

'As you grow older,' answered von Stalhein, rather coldly, 'experience may teach you that it is not wise to put all your, eggs in one basket. The dump is safe where it is. Whatever happens, no one is likely to find it there, or get within hundreds of miles of it. Apart from that, considerable sums of money are involved, and our Roumanian friends had difficulty in getting it out of the country even in instalments.'

'Okay – okay,' retorted Canton. 'I can speak, can't I? I have to fly over that sun-blasted desert, not you. I cross my fingers every time I do the trip.'

'That's what you're paid for,' snapped von Stalhein. 'You'll be doing a longer trip soon.'

'Does that mean the old man has completed his arrangements for the diamond scoop? If so, I suppose he'll want me to do the usual, and get the gen from Alexander Bay?'

'You'll get your orders when the time comes,' said von Stalhein curtly.

'All right. Give me a drink. The air's like an oven over the other side. You ask Luis. He came over with me.'

'I might as well have one, too, while the boys are filling up,' said Groot.

The men all went into the bungalow. Glasses chinked. A cork was drawn.

In the shadow, hardly daring to breathe, Algy listened. After some desultory conversation Groot asked casually, 'How's the new man getting on?'

'All right,' replied Canton. 'He doesn't say much, and what he does say is mostly guff; but I reckon he's the right type. He may sound dumb, but he can fly. I let him take over going out. He knows his stuff.'

'New man! What new man?' Von Stalhein spoke sharply. 'I've heard nothing about a new man. Where is he?'

'Over the other side,' answered Canton. 'The old man told me to take him over right away so that he could carry on with the Hurricane.'

Said von Stalhein, speaking distinctly: 'I particularly asked the Count not to employ any pilot without first letting me see him. He knows nothing about aviation.'

'What's the odds?' came back Canton. A suspicion of sarcasm crept into his voice when he added, 'Have you still got this fellow Bigglesworth on your mind?'

'I know Bigglesworth, you don't,' returned von Stalhein grimly. 'He's a menace, and you'd be wise never to forget it. You say he's been to Australia. Someone has been asking questions in Algeria about the Ahaggar. Put those two facts together, and I don't like the sound of them. The sooner we move our headquarters to behind the Iron Curtain, the sooner I shall sleep comfortably. What's the name of this new man?'

'Smith,' Canton told him. Algy had to strain his ears to catch the answer on account of the noise being made by the mechanics, who were refuelling the Douglas with a mobile motor-driven pump.

'Smith is a convenient name,' said von Stalhein cynically. 'Did you see his passport?'

'No.'

'Why not?'

'He'd lost it.'

The sceptical note in von Stalhein's voice became more pronounced. 'That is sometimes convenient, too. Are you telling me that the Count took on a new man without checking up on his identity?'

Canton laughed shortly. 'Any man likely to be of use to us would probably take good care to lose his identity. We were stuck for another pilot, weren't we?'

'What you mean is, *you* were,' rapped out von Stalhein. 'You were afraid the Count would send you back to the dump to mount guard in the Hurricane.'

'Put it that way if you like,' replied Canton irritably. 'No man in his right mind would want to sit and fry in that hell-hole. I've had one go of it.'

'So you picked up the first pilot to come along? Where did this happen?'

'Nice – at the airport.'

'What was he doing there?'

'Hanging about, flat broke. I found he was a pilot after we'd got talking. He'd lost his wad in the casino at Monte Carlo. He as good as said it wasn't his own money he'd lost, anyway. He may have been on the run, which is as good a recommendation as any. Oh, I sounded him pretty well, don't you worry. I rang up the Count, and he told me to bring him along. *He* engaged him – not me. That's all there was to it.'

'Quite enough, too,' von Stalhein went on sourly. 'The trouble with you is you talk too much. This picking up of new hands casually is dangerous. We're getting slack. It'll lead to trouble, mark my words.'

'I can't see what you're fretting about,' said Canton impatiently. 'This fellow is dumb, anyhow. Just bone from ear to ear, judging from the way he talks.'

'That means nothing,' asserted von Stalhein. 'One of Bigglesworth's men talks more blah than anyone I ever met. As if that isn't enough he fools about with a monocle. He looks and sounds the complete ass – but he isn't.'

'This fellow Smith sports an eyeglass,' said Canton, a suspicion of doubt creeping into his voice for the first time.

There was a brief, stiff silence, before von Stalhein said: 'Describe him.'

Canton gave a fair description of Bertie, which did not surprise Algy, for it confirmed Marcel's story.

'As a matter of fact,' went on Canton, as if he had just remembered something, 'now you put it like that there's been a police Auster in the shed at Nice. I should know. The last time I saw it it was on the tarmac at Gatwick. I was surprised to see it at Nice, because I'd stuck a firework on the exhaust.'

'And you said nothing about this?' grated von Stalhein.

'I didn't see how it could have any connection with us.'

'You didn't see!' Von Stalhein's voice was brittle with accusation. 'You fool! You blundering idiot! It may interest you to know that the man you picked up is Lissie, one of Bigglesworth's best men. There can't be two like him in the world. The Auster being there clinches it. I'll go to Nice and ask a few questions about it. Lissie must have trailed you from England. You picked him up! Don't flatter yourself. He picked *you* up.'

'I wasn't to know,' muttered Canton in a surly voice, in a weak attempt to excuse himself.

'And you took this man to the villa?'

'Yes.'

'Then heaven help you,' said von Stalhein simply. 'The Count will fix you for this. You know how he treats blunderers.'

Anxiety and alarm leapt into Canton's voice. 'Now wait a minute, Erich,' he pleaded. 'I acted for the best, after all. No harm's been done yet. Don't upset the Count. There's no sense in that. I can square things without him knowing anything about it. Give me a break, Erich. Groot will, I know. Lissie – if it is Lissie – and I won't take any chances about that, is safe over the other side. I didn't take my eyes off him till we got there. Those were the Count's orders. He didn't have a chance to speak to a soul. He can't get away. You know the rule about petrol for men on probation? I'll go straight back and fix him.'

There was a short silence as if von Stalhein was considering the matter. 'What are you going to tell the Count? He'll want to know why you went back instead of Groot. He said Groot was to take the machine back.'

'Groot can say he felt sick and I offered to go. You'll do that for me, Groot, won't you? You don't want to go over there?'

Groot agreed.

'If you bump him off, how are you going to account for his disappearance?' inquired von Stalhein.

'I'll say he had an accident. He'll have one, too, I promise you, when I get near him.' Canton's voice was charged with venom.

'How do you feel about it, Luis?' Von Stalhein was apparently speaking to the fourth man.

'P'raps it ees best that way.'

'All right,' consented von Stalhein. 'Perhaps you're right. If the Count learns the truth anything can happen. Make a clean job of it, Canton – and do it as soon as you get there.'

'Leave it to me,' said Canton crisply.

'You'd better be going, then,' answered von Stalhein. 'It'll soon be getting light. You know the Count's orders about not crossing the coast in daylight. And you, Groot, had better push along to the villa, or the stuff will be late. You know how the Count hates being kept waiting.'

'What about Luis?' asked Canton.

'He'll go with Groot. He's due for a spell this side.'

'Okay.'

There was a general movement in the room.

10

A TRIP TO REMEMBER

Algy's state of mind as he listened to this illuminating conversation can be more easily imagined than described. His brain raced in an effort to keep up with it. He knew, now, all that Biggles wanted to know – and more. Yet how, he wondered feverishly, was this knowledge to be applied. How could he get the information to Biggles in time for it to be of any use? Speed was vital. If von Stalhein went to Nice Airport and made inquiries about the Auster it would not take him long to discover that he, not Bertie, had parked it there. He would then know definitely that Biggles was on the trail, and would naturally tell the Count everything, with the result that the leaders, if not the whole crook outfit, would scatter, or fly to an unknown hide-out.

But the overwhelming factor that governed the situation was Bertie's deadly peril. By a casual remark, almost in the nature of a fluke, von Stalhein had learned that he was at El Asile. Algy was in no doubt as to what Canton intended to do. He was going to El Asile – for this was the place obviously meant by 'the other side' – and when he got there he would shoot Bertie forthwith – or kill him somehow. Bertie, unprepared for anything of the sort, wouldn't have a chance. Even if he did escape the initial attack, he would have no hope of getting away, for the waterless desert was a more effective barrier than would have been stone walls or iron bars.

Algy would have liked time to think, but time, at that moment, was a commodity in short supply. He saw that whatever he decided to do would have to be done at once, for the men were already on the move. Once Canton was in the air there could be no stopping him. Bertie would be as good as dead. Could that be prevented, and if so, how?

Algy first considered making off in the Douglas. But that, he saw very soon, was useless. It would tell the men that they had been traced, and perhaps all to no purpose, for it would not prevent Canton from flying out to El Asile in another machine. Von Stalhein might be in radio communication with El Asile, in which case he would certainly warn the people there to be on their guard. The thought of radio worried Algy not a little. His second idea was to wait until Groot and Luis had gone off in the car and then hold up von Stalhein and Canton at the muzzle of his automatic. This thought was induced by the fact that the mechanics, having refuelled the Douglas, were returning to their quarters, so they would not have to be dealt with. But he saw that this was no use either. What if the machine went off before the van departed? Algy's head spun with the speed of these thoughts. In the end he saw that there was only one certain way of preventing Canton from carrying out his intention. It had this advantage, too. If it came off it would leave the others unaware of danger. On this plan he decided.

Crouching low, he made a dash for the machine and got behind it just as the door of the bungalow was opened and the four men came out. For a minute they stood there, talking in low tones; then Groot and Luis went on to the van. Von Stalhein and Canton walked slowly after them, apparently to see them off. This gave Algy the opportunity he needed. The starting of the van smothered the slight noise made by his shoes in the pebbles as he sidled along to the cabin door, got into the aircraft, and lay flat in the afterpart of the empty cabin, where he felt there was little risk of discovery.

After that he could judge what was happening only by sounds. He heard the van drive off, and soon afterwards heard Canton climb into the cockpit. He heard his parting call to von Stalhein. 'Don't worry. I'll fix him.' Then the fuselage quivered as the engines sprang to life. Their growl rose to a bellow. The machine began to move.

Algy took a deep breath of relief. So far so good. There was this about it, he thought. Indecision was a thing of the past. He was now committed absolutely to his adventure. How it would continue would depend on Canton's behaviour when he revealed himself; for he had no intention of allowing Canton to transport him to El Asile, where he would certainly share Bertie's fate. For the time being he was content to sit still, to give the machine time to get clear of the airstrip and gain some altitude. Moreover, he wanted to compose himself, after the shock he had received, to be calm and resolute for the next move. The tricky part of the business was yet to come.

He allowed rather more than half an hour to pass, then got up and looked out of the window. To the east, the first flush of dawn was painting streaks of pallid grey among the stars. Below and ahead lay the Mediterranean, calm, colourless, and deserted. Behind, the coastline of France was a faint indigo smudge. Altitude he reckoned to be about eight thousand feet, with the machine still climbing.

He waited a little longer and then walked forward. Opening the bulkhead door, he could see Canton's head and shoulders. He was well down in his seat, gazing ahead, his right hand resting lightly on the control column.

Knowing that the man would probably be armed, Algy took, as he thought, no chances. It would have been a simple matter to hit the fellow on the back of the head and put him out of action with one blow; but, even though Canton was a potential murderer, if not an actual one, it took more callous toughness than he could muster to strike another pilot so foul a blow. He hoped, foolishly perhaps, and certainly ill-advisedly as things fell out, that Canton would surrender when he saw how matters stood.

Taking out his automatic, he pressed the muzzle firmly between Canton's shoulder blades, and said tersely: 'All right, Canton. The game's played out. Raise your hands and get out of that seat.'

His intention was, when Canton complied, to relieve him of the gun which he suspected he carried, and take over control. Canton did not comply. His body stiffened under the first shock of surprise, which must have been considerable; then, quite slowly, he looked back over his shoulder. For a brief moment their eyes met. Into Canton's dawned recognition. Then they clouded. 'So that police Auster was yours?' he said. 'I should have guessed it.'

'Maybe,' returned Algy coldly.

'Well, I take no orders from cops,' rasped Canton, and before Algy could even begin to suspect his intention he had kicked the rudder-bar and dragged the control column back into his stomach.

The aircraft responded in the manner for which it had been designed. With motors howling, its nose swung up and round in an almost vertical climbing turn. Indeed, it nearly went over on its back. To keep on his feet Algy had to drop his gun and cling to the back of the pilot's seat with both hands; but even so, centrifugal force tore him clear so that he was flung sideways. Canton, who had not troubled to strap himself in, was thrown half into the second pilot's seat and half on the floor; and there for a moment he was held, as was Algy, by the tremendous pressure. Canton, clutching at anything to pull himself up, got hold of the reserve control column, perhaps without realizing what it was; whereupon with its engines roaring protest the machine again nearly stood on its tail.

'You fool!' yelled Algy. 'You'll kill us both!'

Canton's only reply was a wild, hysterical laugh.

Algy managed to gain the pilot's seat and grabbed at the stick to centralize controls, for the machine was hanging on the point of a stall. Canton's hand went to his pocket and pulled out a gun. At that moment the machine stalled, and in no half-measure. With its engines screaming it went down like a bomb. Algy slammed back the throttle and threw himself on Canton, trying to pin his arm. Canton twisted and managed to get his arm free. Algy swung a jab to the jaw and knocked the arm sideways just as the revolver went off. He grabbed the arm and struck again. Canton kicked Algy in the stomach. With a grunt Algy caught Canton's wrist and twisted it so that the revolver fell on the floor.

Inherent stability was now bringing the Douglas out of its stall. The pressure was so great that Algy thought they would both go through the bottom of the machine. Movement was only possible at the absurdly slow rate of a slow-motion film. Canton was reaching for the gun as a child reaches for a toy. Algy, expecting the machine to hit the sea at any moment, got him by the body and hung on. Wrestling in a furious clinch, they got up together, only to fall across the control column. Again the machine, out of control, yawed sickeningly, falling at the same time.

With a sudden jerk Canton tore himself clear and scrambled to the radio transmitter. Algy went after him, ripped the flex from the instrument and knocked Canton into the cabin. His automatic was somewhere on the floor.

He looked for it, knowing that if Canton got it it would be the end. He couldn't see it, so he went on after his man.

The fight was resumed in the cabin, with the machine wallowing like a wounded whale. It must have been obvious to Canton, as it was to Algy, that another minute of this would see the end of both of them. Apparently Canton didn't care. He appeared to have gone mad. Both showing signs of wear, they broke away and glared at each other. Then, seeing that it was a matter of life or death, Algy made a rush. Blows were struck, and in the clinch that followed Canton went down with Algy on top of him. Algy's fist rose and fell viciously. A yard away he saw his automatic lying on the floor. It was no time for squeamishness, so he snatched it up and brought it down on the side of Canton's head. Gasping, without waiting to see the result, he staggered to the window and looked out. The aircraft was gliding steeply towards the sea, now blue and sparkling in sunshine, less than a hundred feet below.

He leapt to the cockpit. Reaching over, for there was no time to get into the seat, he pulled the stick back, and as the machine responded opened up the engines. And there for a few seconds he stood, wild-eyed and panting from shock and exhaustion, while the airscrews clawed their way to a safer altitude. A glance showed Canton lying sprawled on the floor, so he got into the cockpit, found Canton's revolver, and put it in his pocket with the automatic. Still breathing heavily, he took the aircraft up to five thousand feet, put it on a course due south for the time being, and as the machine was trimmed for level flight he was able to leave the controls and return to Canton. He found him in a state of semi-consciousness. In no mood to take any more chances with a man so violent, he used one of his shoelaces to tie his thumbs together behind his back. Then, leaving the bulkhead door open, he returned to the cockpit to take control and decide what next to do.

He knew he was well on his way across the Mediterranean, for ahead and slightly to the west he could see a dark smudge which could only be the island of Minorca. Should he go on to Algiers, or should he turn back to Marseilles? That was the immediate question. Two factors dominated the rest of his deliberations. First, there was Bertie. The immediate danger to him, from Canton, had been dealt with, but there was von Stalhein, who knew he was at El Asile, to be reckoned with. The German was not a man to waste time, and if he did not soon hear from Canton he would take matters into his own hands. Consequently, while Bertie was at El Asile his life would be in peril. The fact that he was unaware of it only made it greater. Secondly, he was desperately anxious to let Biggles know what he himself knew. For this information to be of any use it would be necessary to let Biggles have it before the enemy became aware of what had happened. If von Stalhein went to Nice to make inquiries about the police aircraft it would not take him long to sum up the situation. In that case much would depend on whether the Plaine de la Crau, or the villa, was in radio communication with El Asile. Algy did not know, but it seemed likely. It would be vital for the different units of the organization to keep in touch. If the Douglas did not arrive at El Asile, where presumably it was normally kept, von Stalhein would be informed, reasoned Algy. In that event the whole gang would be on the alert for trouble, and the task of the police in rounding them up would be made much more difficult. The Count, and his head men, would probably take fright and go into hiding. It would be a calamity if, with the game in his hands, that were to happen, pondered Algy moodily. The position still bristled with difficulties. It was not as if the police had only one building to raid. There were at least three widely separated establishments to be dealt with. There might be others that he knew nothing about.

He decided that he ought to go on to El Asile, both for Bertie's sake, and also, by making things appear normal, to prevent the enemy from becoming suspicious. But then there arose the difficulty of Canton. He would have to be disposed of. By arriving at El Asile alone, Algy thought he could concoct a story that might pass; indeed, he could think of no more certain way of arriving there without causing alarm; but obviously he couldn't take Canton. The overriding difficulty was time. Algy wanted to do several things at once. Thus he thought as he went on towards the African coast.

It would, he decided, take too long to go back to Marseilles and try to make contact with Biggles from there – that is, if he was going on to El Asile. There would be explanations at the airport, and delays. There was no real need to go back, anyway. What he could do at Marseilles he would also be able to do at Maison Blanche, the big French airport at Algiers. He would have to land somewhere in order to get rid of his unwelcome passenger. Another important point that he did not overlook was the fact that Marcel was somewhere in North Africa, or should be. Biggles had suggested that he went back there, although whether this advice had been taken he did not know. It would be asking too much to expect to find him at Maison Blanche; but if he was in Algeria he could reasonably expect to locate him at one of the French military or civil aerodromes. He might have gone back to Insalah, his jumping-off place to get the photographs of El Asile.

What Algy really needed more than anything, he perceived, was a contact, someone to whom he could tell his story with a reasonable hope of it being sent home to Biggles, who would then take such steps as he considered necessary in the circumstances. Marcel was the ideal man, if he could be found. It was in the hope of this that he pushed on, on full throttle, for Algiers.

With so much on his mind, that trouble might come from another quarter was the last thing that occurred to him. At any rate, he wasn't looking for it, and consequently, when it came, he was startled almost to the point of panic. If the truth must be told he was half asleep at the time. It is easy to fall asleep in an aircraft, but after his long car drive, his fight with Canton, and his flight afterwards, Algy found it hard to keep awake.

He was approaching the North African coast, a hard blue line straight ahead, when the chatter of machine guns near at hand jerked him to full consciousness. The smack of a bullet striking his machine made him wince. He did not waste time looking for the marksman. His right hand and foot moved automatically, and it was not until the machine was swerving like a startled colt that he looked for the gunner.

It did not take long to find him. Behind and slightly to the right was a Morane. Curiously enough, he did not connect it with Marcel immediately. He was thinking of enemies, not friends. Seeing what was happening, he thought of neither, but concentrated on escape. Not that there was much he could do in the way of evading action with an aircraft so big and heavy. Unable to fight back, he did the next best thing. He put the Douglas in a fairly tight turn and held it there, for in this position he was the least likely to be hit.

His attacker now appeared on the opposite side of the circle, in a turn of the same angle, obviously trying to get on his tail. Algy had a good look at him for the first time; and then, also for the first time, he saw who it was. He recognized the machine, and immediately afterwards, with a curious feeling of unreality at the irony of the situation, the pilot. He had hoped to find Marcel. Instead, Marcel had found him. That was something he had not reckoned on, although Marcel would, of course, be looking for a DC3, Having found it, he was not to be blamed for what he was doing. Having been shot at himself, he had apparently carried out his avowed intention of remounting his guns.

Algy's lips parted in an exasperated smile. First, there was Bertie shooting at Marcel; now Marcel was shooting at him. There seemed to be something awry with their arrangements. However, in the hope of being recognized, he waved. Marcel may not have been looking. If he was he gave no sign of recognition. All he did was tighten the circle and send a stream of tracer bullets across Algy's tail. Algy, still looking at him, saw him gesticulating violently, jabbing a finger downwards.

So that was it, thought Algy. Marcel was ordering him to land. It was an order that he was only too willing to obey, so he side-slipped out of the circle and, throttling back, began a long glide towards the land. Watching in his reflector, he saw Marcel take up a position behind him, as a well-trained dog might shepherd a sheep to its pen.

A quarter of an hour later, when Algy touched down on Maison Blanche airfield, the Morane was still on his tail. He switched off at once. The Morane landed. Marcel jumped down and made for his quarry at a run. As Algy stepped out of the Douglas, Marcel poked a pistol into his ribs. Then, of course, he recognized the man he had captured.

The expression on his face was photographed indelibly on Algy's mind. His eyes opened wide. His lips parted. His lower jaw sagged. He clapped a hand to his forehead, muttering incoherently.

Algy took him by the arm. 'Come on,' he said. 'You're the very man I want to talk to. Where the deuce did you spring from?'

Marcel swallowed and found his voice. 'I am to go to North Africa to find the plane of mystery, Beegles says. I stop at Le Bourget to put on my guns. Then I fly on. All the time I am thinking of the Douglas. Shall I find it? *Voila!* Then in front of me. I see it. *Bon!* Now I say I will catch my man. I catch him. It is you.' Marcel shrugged helplessly. 'I do not understand how this is possible.'

'Come to the canteen and I'll tell you,' promised Algy. 'But first there is another matter. In the cabin I have the man you hoped to catch – the pilot of the mystery plane. I don't want him. I want you to get your friends here to take care of him.'

'It shall be done,' promised Marcel. 'Then what?'

'We shall have to work fast,' answered Algy. 'I'm going on to El Asile to get Bertie, but there's plenty for you to do.'

11

EL ASILE

It was nearly an hour later when Algy took off and headed south for El Asile.

It had been a period of feverish activity. After Marcel had handed Canton over to the police for safe custody, for the moment on a technical charge, over a hasty breakfast Algy told him exactly how matters stood. This information Marcel promised to convey to Biggles with all possible speed. On the back of an envelope Algy made a note, covering the salient points, to be handed to Biggles by Marcel when they met.

Marcel was aghast at the idea of Algy going alone to El Asile, which he said had the appearance of suicide; and it took Algy some time to convince him of the necessity for it. Nothing else, Algy had declared, could save Bertie. What would happen when he got to El Asile, he admitted frankly that he did not know. The next move would depend on what happened when he got there. Nor did he know how he and Bertie would get away from the oasis, although, of course, at the back of his mind there was a vague idea of purloining an aircraft. There could be no question of walking, and there was no other conveyance. They would simply have to rely on their wits, he asserted. Anyway,

Biggles would soon know where they were, and would no doubt take such action as he considered best in the circumstances. There were, he agreed, the villa and the landing-strip at the Plaine de la Crau to be taken into account, although this aspect of the case would naturally be under the direction of the French police. He only hoped that there would be no delay as a result of all these explanations.

Marcel promised that he would do his utmost to speed things up.

The Ahaggar Mountains lie in the Deep Sahara due south of Algiers. The distance, in round figures as the aeroplane flies, is twelve hundred miles. For the early part of this the land is settled, with areas of cultivation; but once the Great Dunes, known as El Erg, are reached, there is nothing ahead but wilderness – the most forbidding desert on earth. Beyond the two French outposts of Insalah and Fort Flatters, lying east and west respectively of Algy's course, civilized life ceases. The only people who can endure the burning sand are the Tuareg Arabs, sometimes known, even to the ordinary desert Arabs, as the Forgotten of God. Otherwise, death and desolation reign undisturbed, and have reigned undisturbed for centuries.

Looking ahead, all Algy could see was a billowing ocean of sand, stretching, it seemed, to eternity. As a spectacle it was awe-inspiring, but it was not a scene on which he, or any other airman, could look without acute anxiety. From now on, he was aware, his life would depend on the reliability of his engines. Should they fail him, all that remained would be a choice of death; a slow one from thirst, or a quick one from a shot from his own pistol. The heat was appalling, and this, with the glare, made flying, except by night, a test of endurance. He could well understand Canton's reluctance to make the trip too often.

The Douglas roared on, Algy's nerves at full stretch, his ears alert to catch the slightest change in the note of his engines. After a while the scene began to change somewhat. Rocks appeared, sometimes singly, sometimes in the form of great outcrops, cracked by the hot hammers of the sun and being slowly reduced to dust by the friction of wind-driven sand. Ahead, needle-pointed crags, sharpened by the same process and looking like the spires of a dead city, cut an ominous horizon. Still farther on Algy saw with relief the twin peaks of Mounts Tahat and Illaman, rising eleven thousand feet above the floor of the desert. He was relieved, because they told him that he was on his course and that his journey was drawing to an end. Before him lay the Ahaggar, a barren world of beetling crags, frowning precipices, and dim mysterious canyons. To all appearances he had arrived at the end of the earth.

He found himself marvelling at the amount of thought that must have gone into the establishment of a base in such a land. Water, it is true, was there, for without it the project could not have been contemplated. But everything else, including petrol, would have to be transported. Only by a regular air lift could such a depot be maintained. But of course, conjectured Algy, if the Count had machines going to and from France regularly, weight carriers like the Douglas, there would be no great difficulty about it. He wondered what sort of men, even for financial reward, would consent to sojourn in such a dreadful place. The answer was soon to be forthcoming, and then he felt that he should have guessed it, for it was the obvious one. He doubted if Biggles, in his views on modern crime and aviation, had imagined anything quite like this; but he had stated that with enough money almost anything was possible. El Asile was an example. The gold that had been stolen from Australia would provide a nice sum to go on with, he reflected.

He had no difficulty in finding his objective, for Marcel had given him the outstanding landmarks. A group of palm-trees and some sparse vegetation were conspicuous, in the absence of anything else green, in a valley. He turned his nose towards it. His hand went to the throttle and at last the steady drone of his motors was broken. As he circled, losing height, he saw men appear from some buildings and look up at him. As they were mostly dressed in white he thought at first they were Arabs. He had no idea of how many men he would find at El Asile, but there were certainly more than he expected.

Wondering what sort of reception he would have, he lowered his undercarriage, landed, and taxied on to where a group of men stood waiting. He saw now that they were not Arabs as he had thought, but white men. As he drew near he scanned their faces anxiously, thinking that from their expressions he would be able to judge if von Stalhein had been in touch with them by radio; but he saw no signs of hostility. He also looked with some concern for Bertie, and smiled faintly when he saw him standing there with the rest.

Algy switched off, climbed down, and walked slowly towards the group. The only face on which there was any sign of recognition was Bertie's, and his expression was so ludicrous that it was all Algy could do to refrain from laughing. All the same, some of the others were looking at him curiously, which was only to be expected. For this he was prepared.

A tall dark man, with a sallow skin and high Slavish cheekbones, stepped forward. 'Who are you?' he asked, first in French, and then in English, presumably to indicate that he was able to talk in either language.

Algy answered in English. 'Lacey's the name. I'm doing the run for Groot, who was to have come.'

'What's happened to Groot?'

'He's gone sick – sunstroke, I fancy. Canton had just done the trip, so the Count sent me.'

'I haven't seen you before?'

'The Count employs a lot of men you've never seen,' alleged Algy casually. 'This is my first trip over this side, and I don't care if I never have to do another.'

'Have any difficulty in getting here?'

'None at all. Groot gave me the course. We were waiting for Canton to come in with the stuff. I'm to take another lot over.'

'Okay. Funny Canton didn't say anything about it. I understood his load was to be the last for some time.'

'Maybe the Count has changed his mind, or else Canton was guessing.'

'How long are you staying?'

'I shall start back tonight.'

'What's the hurry?'

'Those are the orders. I believe another job is coming along pretty soon.'

'I see. You'll find some grub in the kitchen, if you want any?'

'What I really want is some sleep.'

'Make yourself comfortable. One of the boys will show you round. We'll get the stuff on board ready for you.' The man's eyes were on Algy's face. 'What have you been doing? Had an accident, or something?'

Algy had, of course, removed as far as possible, at Algiers, signs of his fight with Canton. Apparently some remained. He smiled lugubriously. 'Some guys in Marseilles tried to get tough with me yesterday,' he explained.

The man nodded and turned away. The onlookers, as hardbitten a crowd as Algy had ever seen, began to disperse. Bertie, who by this time had recovered from what must have been a severe jolt, came over. 'I'll show you the works,' he offered, and together they strolled towards a frame building well inside the shade of the palms.

As soon as they were out of earshot of the rest, Bertie went on: 'I suppose Marcel told you I was here?'

'He did, and was very upset when we didn't believe him.'

'What have you come for?'

'To get you out.'

'But I'm all right, old boy, as right as rain,' protested Bertie.

'You may think so,' returned Algy grimly. 'Von Stalhein is in the gang, and he knows you're here.'

'Does he, by Jove! How very annoying. By the way, how the deuce did you get hold of that kite?'

'It was the only way of getting here. I had to fight Canton to get it. As a matter of detail, he was on his way here to bump you off.'

'Where is he now?'

'At Algiers, in jail. But that doesn't make you safe. You're coming home with me tonight, or you won't get out at all. Von Stalhein won't waste time. I shall push off as soon as it's safe to go. Somehow you will have to get in the machine. I'll leave that to you. There's no other way. Get me a drink. I'm all dried up.'

Bertie disappeared and presently returned with a jug of lemonade, a glass, and some biscuits.

Sitting in the shade of the palms, Algy told him what had happened, concluding with how he had boarded the Douglas, and why. 'How did you get here?' he wanted to know.

Bertie gave his story.

'Have you found out what's going on here?' inquired Algy. Through the trees he noticed some men throwing dust-sheets over the Douglas. 'What's the idea of that?' he inquired, pointing.

'Camouflage, laddie, just camouflage. They realize that there's always a chance of someone flying over, so everything is kept covered up as far as possible. There are more men here than you might think. In fact, I'd say this is the crooks' main depot. My job is to shoot down anyone who gets too nosey. That's why I had to make a show of shooting up poor old Marcel. I knew who it was. With people watching it wasn't easy to find an excuse for missing him, I can tell you. The blokes here don't think much of my shooting. I told them I was a bit out of practice.'

'Tell me this,' requested Algy. 'Are the people here in touch with France by radio?'

'Yes, but they don't use it, for fear of being picked up and traced by the French Security Police, who, they say, have always got an ear to the atmosphere. There are brains behind this show. The radio is only for use in real emergency.' Bertie polished his monocle reflectively. 'The top people don't live here, of course. No bally fear. Too beastly hot. They live where they can enjoy the jolly old fleshpots.'

'What machines have you got here?'

'A spare Douglas, a Mosquito, and a Hurricane. They're parked in a *nullah* at the end of the valley. The petrol-dump is there, too.'

'Shall I have to go there to refuel?'

'No. You'd better not suggest it. You ought to have enough juice on board to get back. Most refuelling is done over the other side, to save hauling it here. They've got a good lot stored here though, in case it's wanted in a hurry. I use a little in the Hurricane. The gang is a bit jumpy because their intelligence service has reported that someone has been asking questions about the White Prophets. That was Marcel, of course. The last thing you'll find here, old boy, is anything to do with religion. They're a lot of bally cut-throats. The head man, the chappie who spoke to you, is Odenski. He's either a Russian or a Roumanian. He keeps the keys, including the keys of the petrol-store. No one can get away. No hope – not an earthly. They only put enough juice in the Hurricane for half an hour. They don't take chances on anyone slipping away. No bally fear. I believe the fellow doing my job before me shot down a couple of French planes that came this way. Then he got fed up and wanted to go home.'

'What happened to him?'

'He's dead – that's all I know.'

'How did you reckon on getting out of here?'

'Hadn't thought about it, old boy. When I got a chance to get in I took it. I didn't think they'd leave me here for ever.'

'Well, now you've got the low-down on the place the sooner we're out of it the better,' declared Algy. 'I've got a feeling the balloon may go up at any moment. If von Stalhein doesn't send it up, Biggles may, when he hears what Marcel has to tell him. I can't guess what Biggles will do, but he'll have more freedom of movement if he knows we're safely out of this trap. How many of these fake prophets are there altogether?'

'About twenty.'

'Great Scott! What do they all do?'

'Nothing, most of them,' answered Bertie. 'One or two of them are mechanics, and some of them, looking really like prophets, or at any rate, priests, go out sometimes. Nobody bothers a priest. They're mostly criminals on the run. They get a safe hide-out for their services. When the police have given up looking for them they're taken out and given jobs to do – still in the gang of course.'

'Which means that the Count plants them where he wants them?'

'That, I fancy, is the idea. They're a lot of disgusting cads, anyway. One of them isn't too bad. A French lad named Emile something or other. We've done quite a spot of chin-wagging. I got most of the gen from him. He's had enough of it here. Been here for goodness knows how long. Suggested we did a bolt together.'

'He might be a spy, testing you.'

'I don't think so, laddie. He got into a spot of bother in Paris, bolted, and joined the Foreign Legion. Hearing his mother was ill, in a weak moment he deserted to see her before she died. She died before he got home. He found the police waiting for him, so the silly young ass bolted again. Somehow the gang got hold of him – by a trick, he says – and sent him here, with the object, no doubt, of using him when the time comes. He's sick to death of the place – got what the French call *le cafard.** Now he wants to go home, give himself up and face the music. But never mind him. What are you going to do now?'

'I'm overdue for some sleep,' asserted Algy.

'Come along to my room and have a nap,' invited Bertie. 'I've been given a corner to sleep in. I'll keep an eye on things.'

'Wake me when it starts to get dark,' requested Algy. 'It's tonight we get out or never. If it came to a showdown we shouldn't have an earthly against this bunch.'

He went with Bertie to his room, one of several small cubicles in the building under the palms. He threw himself down, and in spite of the difficulties and dangers surrounding him, such was his weariness that he was soon asleep. Nor did he wake until Bertie roused him.

'What's the time?' he asked, sitting up.

* Means literally 'the cockroach'. A mental disorder arising from heat, loneliness and boredom.

'Nearly six o'clock,' answered Bertie. 'It'll be dark in a few minutes. It gets dark in this bally place before you know where you are.'

'Is everything quiet?'

'We should have heard about it by now if it wasn't, old boy. The Douglas is ready.'

'What about the dust-sheets?'

'They've pulled them off and loaded up the stuff you're to take back.'

'What is this stuff, do you know?'

'Fertilizer.'

'*What!*' Algy stared.

'That's what they say it is, old boy, and it's marked fertilizer on the sacks. They make the stuff here, anyway. There's a workshop or something which I haven't been allowed to see.'

Algy shrugged. 'Fertilizer, eh? I should never have guessed it.'

'Never mind that now,' replied Bertie. 'It isn't the Australian gold, anyhow. That was in ingots. Tell me, what's the drill for getting away?'

'It seems fairly simple,' answered Algy. 'As soon as it's dark you hide yourself in the Douglas. The best way of doing that is something you'll have to work out for yourself. When I take the machine off I shall assume you're on board. Do you see any difficulty in that?'

'None at all, laddie, as long as nothing happens between now and then to upset the jolly old go-cart. At sundown most of the gang foregather in the canteen to swill hard liquor like the hogs they are. The canteen doesn't open, by order, until six o'clock. Jolly good thing, too, or no one here would ever be sober.'

'I told Marcel that if we got out I should make for Insalah,' informed Algy. 'We should be able to contact Algiers from there to let him know what we're doing.'

'Good enough,' agreed Bertie. 'I'd better drift along now. The blighters might wonder if they saw us too much together. Once the gang gets down to its drinking and gambling they won't see anything, though. By seven there will only be two sober men in camp.'

'Who will they be?'

'The sentries – two of 'em, one at each end of the valley.'

'Sentries! What on earth do they want sentries for in a place like this?'

'I think it's something to do with the Tuareg – you know, the jolly old Arabs who wear blue veils? Pretty wild lot, I believe. Emile tells me there was a bit of a rumpus here a little while ago. Some Tuareg came in asking to fill their water-skins. Some of the bright boys here tried fooling about with their women. Their menfolk objected. Quite properly, too. Whereupon there was a bit of a fuss in which a couple of Arabs were killed. The rest made off. Since then Odenski has mounted a guard, in case they came back.'

'I'll bet von Stalhein doesn't know that, or he'd have been here to see who was responsible,' said Algy seriously. 'That's the last sort of publicity they want.'

'Absolutely. See you later.' Bertie strolled off, unhurriedly, hands in his pockets.

Algy waited until the valley was fast filling with purple shadows and then went out, asking for Odenski. When, presently, the man came, Algy told him he was thinking of moving off. 'Is there anything you want – anything I can bring out next time I come?' he inquired.

Odenski grinned. 'Yes. You can bring over a few cases of brandy. We're always running short.'

Algy laughed. 'I don't wonder at that. It's a thirsty place.'

'I think you'll find everything all right,' said Odenski.

'Thanks.' Algy strolled on to the machine. Out of the corners of his eyes he could see Odenski watching him, but as far as he could gather the man had no suspicion of anything being wrong. There was no sign of Bertie, so he could only hope that he was on board. He was about to climb into the cockpit when there was a hail behind him. Looking round he saw Odenski with an arm raised.

Seeing him turn, Odenski called: 'Better wait a minute. What's this coming?'

Algy inclined his head, and his heart missed a beat as his ears caught the drone of an aircraft, obviously low and travelling on full throttle. He, too, wondered what was coming; and he had an uneasy feeling that it was no harbinger of peace. He could see nothing, for the sun had dipped below the horizon and darkness was dropping from the sky. Odenski had turned, and was staring up the valley, so he climbed quietly into his seat. And there he had to wait, staring through the windscreen, for the other aircraft was coming straight down the valley, the direction in which he was facing and would have to take off. To take off, therefore, would be to invite a head-on collision; indeed, there was such an obvious likelihood of this that he dare not move. Stiff with annoyance and impatience, for another minute would have seen him safe in the air, he could only sit and watch. However, perceiving that urgent action might be called for, he took a chance and started his engines. Odenski heard this, of course, and signalled to him to stay where he was. Algy opened the side window and waved back to show that he had no intention of moving.

The oncoming machine loomed suddenly in the gloom. Algy recognized a Mosquito. He hoped that it would make a circuit before coming in, for if it did he would snatch the opportunity to get off. But it did nothing of the sort. It came in straight down the valley, landed, and ran to a stop directly in front of him. Algy's lips went dry, for if the machine remained there it would be impossible for him to do anything. He breathed again when the Mosquito taxied on a little way before switching off, coming to a standstill a little to his right. A man dropped out. It was von Stalhein. Another followed. Algy recognized Groot.

Von Stalhein's business was obviously so urgent that he could not wait until he had reached Odenski before he spoke. He shouted. 'Is Canton here?'

'No,' answered Odenski.

'Have you seen him?'

'No.'

'Then the report we had was right,' declared von Stalhein. 'The police have got him.' He swung round and pointed to the Douglas. 'Who brought that machine here?'

'A new man. Fellow named Lacey.'

'Where's Lacey now?' Von Stalhein fired the words.

Odenski pointed at the Douglas. 'He's just going back.'

In a second a pistol was in von Stalhein's hand. He ran towards the Douglas. Groot ran to get in front of it. But Algy's hand was on the throttle, and he banged it open. He ducked instinctively as he saw von Stalhein's hand go up. He saw the flash of the shot, but the sound of it was drowned in the roar of his motors.

The machine moved forward, all too slowly for Algy, for both von Stalhein and Groot were shooting at him, and he held his breath until he judged that he was out of range. Two bullets at least struck the machine, for at such close quarters the big target could hardly be missed. Where they went he did not know. As it reached flying speed the machine rose ponderously; but he held the control column forward, for it was speed he wanted, not height.

He was staring into the darkness ahead when Bertie appeared beside him.

'I say, old boy, that was a bit hot, wasn't it?' said Bertie cheerfully, dropping into the reserve pilot's seat.

'Too hot,' answered Algy shortly, for his nerves were on edge. 'If someone comes after us in the Hurricane it'll be even hotter.'

'Its tanks are only a quarter full.'

'That may get it far enough to do the dirty on us.'

'If it can find us, laddie, if it can find us. She's under her dust-sheets, and it'll take a little while to get 'em off.'

'That Mosquito may have guns on it.'

'True enough, old boy,' admitted Bertie, still cheerful. 'Keep her low and give her the works. They'll have a job to spot us against the ground.'

'I'd rather they spotted us than we bumped into a mountain.'

'We'll soon be clear of the rocks.'

'The sooner the better. Where did those shots go?'

'One came jolly close to me,' declared Bertie. 'Made me jump, I can tell you.'

'I was thinking about the machine. Can you see anything behind us?'

Bertie looked. 'Not a bally thing,' he reported.

'Good.'

The machine roared on. Ahead lay the desert, sombre and still, like a rough sea suddenly frozen while in motion.

They had settled down in their seats when, without warning, a voice behind them spoke, spoke in a tone pitched high with alarm. It said one word. '*Essence!*'

Badly startled, Algy and Bertie turned round together. A dark form with a pallid face could be seen vaguely against the bulkhead.

'It's Emile,' said Bertie. 'Phew! My word, laddie, you gave me a fright!'

'*Essence!*' shouted the lad.

'How did *he* get here?' demanded Algy, crossly.

Bertie put the question to the boy and ascertained that, thinking the machine was going to France, he had stowed himself away.

'Why does he keep on shouting petrol?' asked Algy. Even as he asked the question he sniffed, and understood. 'Take over,' he told Bertie curtly, and going aft, was met by a cloud of petrol spray. He returned quickly to the cockpit. 'The main tank has been holed,' he said, almost viciously. 'One of von Stalhein's shots did it, no doubt. It's squirting like a soda-water syphon. See if you can do anything about it. If you can't, we've had it.'

12

BIGGLES TAKES A TURN

Ginger, checking lists of Douglas DC3 registration marks in the Operations Room at Gatwick, was browned off, and made no secret of it. 'It isn't like you to sit here and let other people do the work,' he told Biggles reproachfully. 'Isn't it about time I did something, anyway?'

'I may need you here,' Biggles told him serenely. 'A commanding officer is entitled to an aide-de-camp to help him out with the odd jobs,' he went on banteringly. 'As for me, I can't be in several places at once. I have to be somewhere where I can be kept in touch with what's going on. To change the subject, it looks rather as if Marcel's mystery plane is one of the two DC3s that are supposed to have gone down in the Atlantic some time ago.'

Ginger was not to be put off. 'To return to the subject,' he persisted, 'I can't imagine what everyone's doing. Not a word from any of them. I'd say they're all having a thundering good holiday in the sunshine, bathing, and all that.'

'If Bertie's at El Asile he won't be doing much bathing,' averred Biggles sarcastically. 'It'll probably take him all his time to get enough liquid to shave with. I'll admit there's something a bit queer about their silence. If we don't soon hear from one of them you'd better dash down to find out what's going on.'

The telephone rang. 'Here's one of them now,' said Ginger optimistically as he picked up the receiver. His face fell as he listened for a moment and then put a hand over the mouthpiece. 'It's the Air Commodore,' he told Biggles. 'He wants to know if there are any fresh developments.'

'Tell him I've nothing fresh to report,' requested Biggles. 'I'll let him know as soon as I have any news myself.'

Ginger conveyed the message and hung up.

Hardly had he done so than the bell jangled again. 'Now what?' he muttered irritably, hand on the receiver. Then he stiffened and his eyes switched meaningly to Biggles. 'Long distance,' he said tersely. 'Hello – yes?' he called. 'Hang on, he's here.' His attitude had changed when, holding out the instrument, he turned to Biggles. 'Here we are at last. It's Marcel on the line. He's speaking from Marseilles. He sounds more on his toes than usual.'

Biggles took over the telephone. 'Hello, Marcel,' he greeted. 'Yes, I'm listening. Go ahead.'

He sat for so long without speaking, with the instrument to his ear, that Ginger, without a clue as to what was being said, fidgeted with impatience.

At last Biggles spoke. 'Great work, Marcel. All right. I'll be there. I'll get off right away. Goodbye.' He hung up and swung round in his chair. 'You've got your wish,' he told Ginger. 'This is where we get mobile.'

'What on earth was all that about?' demanded Ginger.

'Get a grip on yourself, and I'll tell you,' answered Biggles. 'Things are humming. Here's the position as I understand it from Marcel. Bertie is at El Asile. Algy is on his way there to get him out, having pinched the mystery Douglas for the job. He got the machine at one of the enemy's secret refuelling stations in the South of France.

Guess who was in charge of it? No – don't bother, I'll tell you. Von Stalhein.'

Ginger's eyes went round. 'Then he *is* in it?'

'Apparently. By a bit of bad luck he discovered that Bertie had got into El Asile. Canton was to go down in the Douglas and bump him off. Algy heard this and jumped the plane. It seems that he and Canton fought it out in the aircraft. Algy won, and Canton is in quod at Algiers. Algy told Marcel all about it at Maison Blanche. Then he went on to El Asile, leaving Marcel to give me the gen. The Villa Hirondelle seems to be the headquarters of the gang in Europe. The big boss is a German named Count von Horndorf. There's reason to suppose the swag is kept at El Asile and brought over to the villa as required. It's unloaded near Marseilles and goes on to Eze by road. That's the gist of it. The job now becomes one for the French police, as the racket is being run from their territory; but as we've handled the thing so far they want our co-operation. We've an interest in the Australian gold, anyway. Marcel has told his chief in Paris how things stand, with the result that Captain Joudrier of the *Sûreté* is flying straight down to Marseilles, where Marcel is to meet him. They're going to wait for us there. I've met Joudrier. He's efficient, and can be relied on to keep pace with any situation that arises. His idea is to make a quick raid on von Stalhein's dump first, and then go on to the villa at Eze. Having cleaned them up, he'll go straight on to El Asile. In this way he hopes to mop up the whole gang before they can re-organize. It seems to me that he's taking a bit of a risk, because if he doesn't find any stolen property at the villa it's hard to see what he can charge these people with, apart from trivial offences like using a government airfield without permission. Maybe he intends to grab them while he can, and hold them until we can produce evidence to prove what they were doing. Of course, if we can find some of that Australian gold, that'll be all the evidence he needs.'

'What about Algy and Bertie?'

'They'll have to take care of themselves until we can get to them. I gather from Marcel that if Algy can get Bertie out of El Asile he'll make for Insalah and wait there until he hears from us. The sooner we're at Marseilles the better. We mustn't keep Joudrier waiting. Tell Smyth to pull out a Mosquito and get our small kit on board while I tell the Air Commodore what's cooking.'

'Okay.' Ginger departed in some haste.

Ten minutes later the Mosquito was in the air, heading south at top speed.

It was five o'clock when its wheels touched the dusty airfield of Marignane, the big airport for Marseilles; and signs of police activity were evident even while the machine was running in. Two big cars were standing on the tarmac, and near them a little group of gendarmes. Two men, one in uniform, were standing a little apart, looking at a map. Ginger recognized Marcel. The other, he supposed – correctly – was Captain Joudrier. As the Mosquito switched off they put the map away and walked forward to meet the occupants. A minute later Biggles was shaking hands with Joudrier, to whom Ginger was introduced.

Little time was lost, and none wasted, for the French detective made it clear that he was anxious to strike before the crooks, through their intelligence service, could get wind of the impending raid. The cars, he said, were waiting. Everything they were likely to want was in them. The disused aerodrome on the Plaine de la Crau was the first objective. There would be no difficulty about finding it, because he had studied a map provided by the French Air Ministry.

Joudrier went on to say that he had first considered making the raid by air; but there were difficulties that made this inadvisable, one being that he was anxious to catch the enemy unprepared, which would be impossible if aircraft were used. In any case, the Plaine de la Crau was no great distance away, so little time would be lost by using fast cars. With this Biggles was in full agreement. 'I am ready when you are,' he said.

Captain Joudrier took the wheel of the leading car. With him went Biggles, Ginger, Marcel and two gendarmes. Eight more gendarmes packed themselves into the second car.

Darkness was closing in as Joudrier set off at a speed that made Ginger push his feet into the floor. The direction was north-west, for Marignane Airport lies halfway between Marseilles and the Plaine de la Crau.

Of the villages through which they flashed Ginger saw little. The country was flat, uninteresting, and unknown to him; but the driver obviously knew where he was going, for not once did he slacken speed until they left the main road, taking the track which, although Ginger was not to know it, was the same one taken by Algy when he had followed the van. All lights were now switched off, and eventually, when the track ended, the cars pulled in against the cypresses that guarded the ruins of the cottage. Here Algy's car was found. It was responsible for a short delay while guesses were made as to whom it belonged and what it was doing there. There was nothing, of course, to indicate that it had been put there by Algy; but Marcel, who knew more of the details of Algy's adventures than anybody, said he thought it must be his. They left it there, and in deepening darkness went on quietly on foot.

As soon as the dilapidated aerodrome buildings loomed up against the sky, Captain Joudrier deployed his men with the confidence born of experience. Two lines of gendarmes, pistols in hands, went out in an encircling movement. Ten minutes elapsed, and then all precautionary measures were abandoned. A single blast on a whistle and the men closed in swiftly.

'Watch for von Stalhein,' Biggles told Ginger tersely. 'He's the man we want.'

What happened after that was not easy to see. There were shouts and the usual sounds of panic flight. A shot was fired. There was a babble of voices. When the cordon closed right up it was found that six men, protesting volubly, had been caught in the net. Von Stalhein was not among them.

A quick search was made. It concentrated, of course, on the bungalow, which was found to be furnished comfortably and showed signs of recent occupation. But von Stalhein was not in it. Nor had he been in it when the raid was launched, Joudrier asserted, for it would have been impossible for anyone to get through the cordon without being seen.

'We will soon settle the matter,' declared the detective, and ordered the captured men, now in handcuffs, to be brought before him. At first they were inclined to be surly, and refused to speak; but when Joudrier recognized two of them as felons wanted by the police, the nerve of one of them, a Polish ex-taxi driver of Paris, broke, and under Joudrier's brittle interrogation he said he was ready to talk – presumably in the hope of improving his position.

Actually, he hadn't much to tell, for the simple reason, as soon became evident, that he knew little about the real business of the gang, for which he worked as a mechanic. One thing he did reveal, however, was highly important, for it answered a pressing question. Von Stalhein, he alleged, had gone 'over the other side', earlier in the day, although for what purpose he did not know. He had gone in a Mosquito. He knew where he had gone, said the man, on account of the quantity of petrol carried.

Ginger realized that this, in view of what he knew, was probably the truth. Anyway, it accounted for von Stalhein's absence.

On being further questioned the Pole admitted reluctantly that by 'the other side' he meant El Asile. He knew about the place because he had spent some time there.

With that, for the moment, Joudrier was satisfied. He ordered the men to be taken to Marseilles, detailing four of his men for the purpose. Two others were ordered to take charge of the landing ground and arrest anyone landing on it.

Captain Joudrier and Biggles now had a quick conference, with Ginger and Marcel standing by. No change of plan was proposed. The Villa Hirondelle remained next on Joudrier's list for investigation, and with this Biggles was in accord. There was, however, no need for him to go there, he pointed out. There was nothing he could do. Joudrier did not need his help. He was, he said, worried by the significance of von Stalhein's sudden departure for El Asile. It might have something to do with Algy and Bertie, on whose account he was therefore rather worried. He would, if Joudrier had no objection, return to Marseilles with Ginger, and go straight on to Insalah. If he found Algy and Bertie there he would wait for Joudrier and his men to join them. The raid on El Asile could then be made.

Joudrier thought this was a good arrangement.

The question of Marcel then arose, and he himself suggested the answer. It was that he should fly on to Nice and wait there for Joudrier to pick him up. After the raid on the villa he would be able to fly out to Insalah straight away and inform Biggles of any discovery that might have an effect on the situation.

This was so obviously a practical and useful way of employing him that it was agreed to without argument.

Joudrier said he would go on to Eze by road. He was not equipped for transporting by air the large number of men he would need to surround the grounds of the Villa Hirondelle. He would be able to fly only as far as Nice anyway, and from there employ road transport. So the loss of time in going by road would be very little, and unlikely to make any difference to the result.

These arrangements having been agreed, steps were taken forthwith to put them into action.

13

SMOKE IN THE SAHARA

Another day was being born in a blaze of colour when Biggles and Ginger, weary after their long flight, landed at Insalah.

After the decisions reached with Joudrier and Marcel on the Plaine de la Crau they had returned to Marignane, where, while the tanks of their Mosquito were being topped up, they took the opportunity to snatch a meal. A night flight across the Mediterranean followed, and as Biggles had no intention of being caught in the desert short of fuel, the tanks were again topped up at Maison Blanche airport. There was a little delay here, as although Biggles' police credentials smoothed the way, there were certain formalities that could not be brushed aside. However, the Mosquito was soon on its way again, kicking the cool night air behind it as it headed south for the Equator. Ginger took a turn at the controls, giving Biggles a rest; then Biggles took over again, and Ginger slept the rest of the way. He was, in fact, asleep, when Biggles nudged him to announce that Insalah was below and he was going down.

Yawning, Ginger saw that another day had dawned, although from the position of the sun, which was still low, it was not very old. A glance at the watch on the instrument panel told him that it was a few minutes after six o'clock.

The officers and men stationed at the lonely outpost were already on the move, for in desert countries this is the only hour of daylight when it is possible to do any serious work without discomfort. Biggles and Ginger were greeted courteously by the commandant, who informed them that he had heard something of what was going on from Marcel, who had been there making inquiries.

As soon as the conventional formalities had been observed Biggles asked after Algy, and was disappointed to learn that nothing had been seen of him or Bertie. He had hoped – indeed expected – to find them waiting there, and looked worried when he learned they had not arrived. These hopes were not based entirely on the matter of their personal safety: he was relying on their report to put him in a position to tell Joudrier what opposition might be expected at El Asile when the oasis was raided. He had reckoned on learning a good deal about the place. However, they were not there, so, as he told Ginger presently, all they could do was wait.

'It looks as if they weren't able to get out last night, in which case they must still be at El Asile,' he observed. 'However, they might show up any minute now. It's no use going on to the oasis by ourselves; we should probably do more harm than good. Before we can tackle the place we shall have to wait for Joudrier to come.'

They were given the usual light French breakfast of coffee and rolls, after which there was nothing for them to do except try to keep cool and control their impatience.

At noon Marcel arrived, having flown direct from Nice, with news that he lost no time in narrating. It did nothing to raise the spirits of the listeners. The villa had been raided, with disappointing results. The Count must have been away at the time, or had a secret exit. At all events, he wasn't there. Some servants had been arrested and taken away for further questioning. No gold had been found, nor anything else of an incriminating nature. Nor did there appear anything in the way of a link with the Plaine de la Crau, for which reason Joudrier was upset, as unless something turned up he would have no charge against the men he had arrested. Among the people from the villa there was a deserter from the Army, but that was a trivial offence compared with what had been anticipated. The search was still going on when Marcel left. There was a safe, which, up to that time, it had not been possible to open. It was a small one, and Joudrier had little hope of finding any of the Australian gold in it. The van was there, but this was another disappointment. Marcel smiled wanly. 'All that we found in it were some small bags of fertilizer.'

Biggles stared. 'Fertilizer!'

'Just dirty black dust. The bags have the name printed on them – fertilizer.' Marcel shrugged. 'That is what they say. It is the stuff which you would call basic slag. It comes from iron furnaces. It is put on lawns to make the grass grow nicely.'

'That sounds a funny tale to me,' said Biggles suspiciously.

'You think it may be what you would call a blind – *hein*?'

'You say Algy told you he saw some bags of stuff being unloaded from the Douglas at the Plaine de la Crau?' questioned Biggles.

'That is what he told me.'

'And he saw these bags put in the van?'

'Yes.'

'What would the Count want with fertilizer? And even if he did want it, why should he haul it about in an aeroplane? Does that make sense to you?'

'No.'

'Nor me,' asserted Biggles. 'But never mind that for the moment. I'll think about it. Did you have any difficulty in getting into the villa?'

'No. The dogs were thrown pieces of liver with something on it to make them sleep. Then we cut through the fence. We go to the house. Joudrier knocks on the door. When it is opened we rush in. It is so simple.'

'And you've no other news?'

'Only that Joudrier is coming here with many men, in a big transport which he requisitioned at Marignane. He is mad to capture El Asile, for there he hopes to find things which will put the gang into prison. He thinks perhaps the Count is there.'

'So after all that we've no evidence that these men did the job in Australia?' said Biggles moodily.

'That is true,' admitted Marcel, in a melancholy voice.

'I can well believe that Joudrier is worried,' said Biggles. 'I'm worried too, if it comes to that, because it was on our information that the raids were made. Still, I'm sure he was right to strike when he did. Had he waited he might have lost sight of the whole bunch. When does Joudrier reckon to get here?'

'He thinks he will be here before it is dark.'

Biggles nodded. 'The sooner the better. I'm getting worried about Algy and Bertie. I can't help feeling that had nothing gone wrong they would have been here by now. Anyhow, there it is. There's nothing more we can do. The Commandant has insisted that we accept his hospitality while we're here, so we might as well go and have some lunch. Eat when you can is a good plan on jobs like this. Not that I want much. The heat certainly is terrific.'

It was in the middle of the afternoon that the Commandant, looking grave, brought news that put Biggles on his feet. His manner was that of one who brings disturbing intelligence. It turned out to be even worse than Ginger expected.

The Commandant explained that he had received a message which he thought might have some bearing on the business that had brought them there. The pilot of a French airliner coming up from Lake Chad had seen an aircraft, which he thought was a Douglas transport plane, down in the desert not far from the Ahaggar. He was unable to pinpoint it exactly, but it was roughly on a line between the Ahaggar and Insalah. He had flown over it very low, but had seen no signs of life. As far as he could judge the machine had not crashed, but appeared to be in good order. He had not dared to risk a landing, as he was carrying a full load of passengers, whose lives he dare not hazard. All he could do was send out a signal on his radio, to Algiers, in case a plane was overdue. What, concluded the Commandant, would Biggles like him to do about it?

'This must be the machine I'm waiting for, Monsieur le Commandant,' said Biggles. 'It went to El Asile from Algiers and was to come on here. I hoped it would be here before I arrived. There is only one thing to do. I'll fly out and look at this machine.'

The Commandant did not demur. All he said was: 'You do not need me to tell you that to land in the desert is an operation attended by much danger. At this hour the heat strikes, as my men say, like the hammers of hell.'

'I am aware of that, Monsieur le Commandant,' answered Biggles. 'But the men who landed that machine may have been my friends, so I must go.'

'But assuredly,' confirmed the Commandant. He had more than once been faced with the same situation.

Biggles looked at Marcel. 'If Joudrier comes before I get back tell him what has happened. What action he takes I am content to leave to his discretion; but you can say

I think he would be wise to proceed with the plan, as it was decided, without waiting for me.'

'The Commandant can tell him this,' said Marcel. 'Me, I shall go with you,' he announced, quite definitely.

Biggles argued against this on the grounds that it was taking an unnecessary risk.

The Commandant intervened. He said he thought it would be a good thing if Marcel went. He should not land, but remain in the air to watch what happened. If for any reason Biggles was unable to get off the ground, Marcel would at least know where he was, in which case he would arrange for water to be dropped to him. He had special equipment for that sort of emergency, he said.

This was so obviously a sensible arrangement that Biggles acknowledged it, and submitted. 'All right. If we're going we might as well get off right away,' he opined.

Ten minutes later the Mosquito and the Morane took off into the glare of the heat-tortured atmosphere, and took up a course for the estimated position of their objective.

Hardly a word was spoken either by Biggles or Ginger as they bored through the quivering air. There was really nothing to talk about. The situation was plain enough, and no amount of guessing would produce the answer to the question, why had the machine landed in the desert? This was something close investigation would no doubt reveal. The Mosquito, fast though it was, rocked as it cut through currents of air that rose and fell according to the nature of the terrain below.

On the open desert, with hardly a mark on its shimmering surface to catch the eye, the task of finding the Douglas should be a comparatively easy one, thought Ginger. And so it proved. Flying at five thousand feet, as soon as the crests of the Ahaggar appeared ahead, Biggles began quartering the ground in ten-mile-long casts. While on one of these Ginger touched him on the arm and pointed. There was no need to say anything. There, on an area of sand as flat as if it had been rolled, a Douglas stood in flying position on its three wheels. Its shadow, creeping like an inky stain from under it as the sun dipped in the west, was more conspicuous than the machine.

Biggles made only one remark as he glided down towards it. 'I don't think it could have been forced down, because whoever was flying it obviously had time to pick a landing ground.'

'I can't see anything wrong with it,' observed Ginger.

Biggles flew low over the aircraft, dreading what he might see. But nothing like a body was in sight, on the ground or in the cockpit. After a careful survey of the ground he put the Mosquito down and taxied right up to the abandoned aircraft. There was no longer any doubt about it being abandoned, because had anyone been there he would have shown himself. Ginger realized that if Algy or Bertie was there, he could only be in the cabin, dead or unconscious.

The Mosquito had hardly stopped moving when Biggles was down, running. Ginger was at his heels. Marcel circled overhead.

Half a minute was ample time to provide the answer to the one question that really mattered. Neither Algy nor Bertie was there, inside the machine or out of it. Nor was there anyone else.

Biggles investigated, while Ginger tried to convey the news to Marcel by means of signals. When Biggles got out of the Douglas he said: 'This machine was shot at. The main tanks were holed. That could have happened either in the air or on the ground, but I fancy it must have been on the ground.'

'Why?'

'Because had it been shot at in the air the weapon used would have been a machine gun, in which case there would almost certainly have been several holes – unless, of course, the range was very long, giving the bullets time to spread. Moreover, the shots were fired from below the machine, not above it.'

'You think it could have happened at El Asile?'

'It could, but I can't say it did. It could have happened when Algy was on his way out, or on his way home. On his way out he would have been alone, of course; on his way home he'd have Bertie with him, because he wouldn't start without him. One thing is certain. The enemy knew the machine wasn't being handled by one of their own men or they wouldn't have shot at it.'

'Shots were fired in the machine, apparently, when Algy and Canton were fighting.'

'Yes, but Algy landed at Maison Blanche after that. The tanks weren't leaking then.'

'If Algy and Bertie were in this machine, and had to force-land on the way home, why didn't they stand by, knowing that we should be along? They must have known we'd come after the information Algy gave Marcel to pass on to you.'

Biggles shook his head. 'I don't know. They must have been losing petrol fast, and being afraid they couldn't get home, perhaps went down to plug the leak.'

'Could the people of El Asile have followed them, and captured them?'

'I don't think so. There are strong arguments against that,' returned Biggles. 'Had Algy and Bertie been cornered here they would have put up a fight rather than be captured. There wasn't a fight. If there had been there would be expended cartridges lying about. I can't see one. Again, if they *were* captured, I question if they'd be taken to El Asile, or anywhere else. They would have been shot here. They would certainly have been shot. Why take them to El Asile to shoot them?'

'All right,' resumed Ginger. 'Let's assume that Algy, or Bertie, or both of them were in this machine when it came down. They might not have had any water with them. They'd soon be desperate for some. I mean, could they have gone off to look for water?'

Biggles lit a cigarette. 'I can't see that happening. Algy's not a fool. He'd realize the risks of getting lost. Besides, he'd know there was no water about except at El Asile. He'd soon work out that his best chance was to stick to the machine, knowing that one of us would be along and would be pretty certain to spot him. The most puzzling thing to me is this. If there wasn't a fight, they must have gone away of their own accord. That being so, why didn't they leave a message, just a scrap of paper, to let us know what they intended doing?'

Ginger gazed across the hopeless landscape. If he sought inspiration from it he found none. 'We can't be a great way from El Asile,' he observed. 'I suppose they wouldn't attack it on their own?' He spoke without much confidence.

'Not unless they were raving mad, and I see no reason why they should be.'

'Well, what are you going to do about it?'

'I'm going to look for them,' decided Biggles. 'We can't just do nothing. If they left here on their feet, and I don't see how else they could have gone, they won't be far away.'

'And if we can't spot them?'

'I shall go to El Asile. If they're there, and still alive, it won't be for long. It's up to us.'

'There's only about an hour of daylight left.'

'That should be enough.'

'What about Joudrier? If he's arrived at Insalah he'll be annoyed if we keep him waiting.'

'We shall have to let him know what's happened.'

'How?'

'I'm going to bring Marcel down and send him back. There's no risk in landing here.' Biggles walked into the open and made beckoning signals to the Morane, still cruising overhead.

Marcel soon saw what was required of him, and came down. He taxied up. 'What happens?' he questioned eagerly.

'That's what we'd like to know,' answered Biggles. 'There's no one here.' He explained the situation briefly. 'I want you to go back and tell Joudrier how we're fixed,' he concluded. 'Tell him to carry on without me. He might come this way. If we're still here I'll make a signal. If there's no signal he'll probably find me at El Asile.'

Marcel looked startled, then resigned. 'El Asile! If you are shot I will make a nice tombstone for you,' he promised sadly. He shrugged. 'As if there are not enough graves in the desert already.'

Biggles smiled and patted him on the shoulder. 'That's kind of you, *mon ami*. The thought will comfort me when I'm dodging bullets. Now forget about things like that. Go back and tell Joudrier that I'm sorry things seem to be getting in a tangle, but we'll have them all buttoned up at the finish.'

'*Bon!*' Without another word Marcel strode back to his Morane and took off.

'The more I see of Marcel, the more I like him,' remarked Biggles, as he turned to the Mosquito. 'I shall cover the district as far as seems reasonable, working towards the oasis,' he explained. 'If we see nothing by sundown I shall go on to El Asile.'

'You mean, you're going to land there?'

'I wouldn't expect to see much from up topsides.'

Ginger was staring at the horizon. 'Is that a cloud I can see?' he asked wonderingly. 'Don't tell me it's going to *rain!*'

Biggles looked long and steadily at the object to which Ginger had called attention. 'That isn't a cloud,' he said slowly. 'They don't have such things there. It's smoke. Smoke over the Ahaggar. We'll have a closer look at that presently. Come on, we're wasting daylight.'

14

ENEMIES OR ALLIES?

For an aircraft, a punctured petrol tank is a serious matter at any time; if it occurs when the machine is flying over such an area of the earth's crust as Algy and Bertie knew was beneath them, then the expectation of life for the occupants becomes very slim indeed.

In the Douglas DC3 there are two main fuel tanks located forward of the centre-section spar. Just where the machine had been damaged Algy did not know; all he knew was the floor was swimming with petrol, and blinding spray, ejected under pressure, made it impossible to discover where it was coming from. Emile had been forced to leave the cabin to escape asphyxiation. Bertie groped his way in, but retired quickly with his hands over his eyes, in considerable pain. It was not possible to check, except over a period of time, the rate at which petrol was being lost; but as the machine had not been refuelled since it started on its outward journey it seemed unlikely that it would get far.

That was not the only danger. There was another, even more alarming. The aircraft was fast becoming soaked with petrol. The cabin was charged with petrol vapour, and it would need one spark only to cause it to explode. When

Algy looked at the glowing gases streaming from his exhausts, lurid, as they always are in the dark, and unpleasantly close, his mouth went dry.

There was no question of plugging the hole, or holes, even if they could be located. In fact, it was impossible to do anything about the trouble while the machine was in flight and while darkness persisted. The alternatives seemed to be, to risk fire and carry on as long as the machine would remain airborne, or go down on the first level ground that presented itself and wait for daylight, when a temporary repair might be effected. The trouble was, Algy saw, that if he chose the former course and went on, the engines might fail for want of fuel at a place where a crash would be inevitable. Even a minor crack-up might well cause an explosion, because a dying magneto has an unpleasant habit of throwing a last spark.

Algy put the matter to Bertie, whose life was at stake as well as his own. There was no need to explain the situation, because Bertie was just as well aware of it as Algy.

'I'd go down, old boy,' said Bertie without hesitation, really serious for once. 'There are plenty of flat patches. I noticed them on the way here.'

'If we strike soft sand we may never get off again,' Algy pointed out.

'Biggles or Marcel will spot us when they go to the oasis. We're right on their course.'

'Von Stalhein may spot us first if he comes looking for us.'

'I'd risk that, laddie. I'd rather face von Stalhein than stay up here and be fried. I can't see us getting to Insalah, so we might as well go down at once.'

Algy said no more. Everyone has a horror of fire. An airman probably has a greater horror of it than most people, because in spite of all precautions he sees too many machines end their careers in flames. The strain of flying a machine charged with an explosive mixture of petrol gas is severe; so Algy was satisfied to accept Bertie's decision. His eyes explored the desert, a bare five hundred feet below, seeking an area free from obstructions.

'There you are, old boy – half left!' exclaimed Bertie sharply. 'There's a spot there that looks just the job.'

Algy made a flattish turn, eased the stick forward and throttled back. He also burnt his boats, so to speak, by cutting the ignition. The noise of the engines died abruptly. With stationary propellers the Douglas dropped towards the earth like a phantom, a shadowy wraith on which the wan light of a rising moon played strange tricks. No one spoke. Algy lowered his undercarriage. A minute of breathless suspense followed. If the sand turned out to be soft – and this is a factor which from the air, even in daylight, it is impossible to determine – the wheels would plough in and cause the machine to overturn.

The wheels touched with a gentle bump, and Algy's nerves relaxed as they trundled on. Almost without a sound they rolled on over firm ground, the machine losing speed slowly and finally coming to a standstill.

'Nice work, laddie,' congratulated Bertie. The words came strangely clear and loud in the solemn hush that had fallen.

'Let's get clear and have a cigarette,' suggested Algy. 'I'm all of a dither.'

They all got out. Having put a safe distance between them and the machine, they sat down. Algy took out his cigarette case. 'You chose a bad moment to start hitchhiking,' he told Emile, with grim humour.

Emile's only answer was a shrug. Hands in his pockets, he gazed unperturbed across a landscape, with which his life in the Foreign Legion had no doubt made him familiar.

'I don't think there's anything we can do until it gets light enough to see the damage,' remarked Algy.

'Not a bally thing,' agreed Bertie. 'No use striking matches, or anything like that.'

'When it gets light we shall be able to see what juice we have left.'

'Absolutely. This is a pretty lonely spot – what?'

No one answered. The moon rose clear of the horizon, flooding the scene with blue light and revealing the desert in all its naked desolation.

'There is this about it,' went on Bertie presently. 'We're pretty conspicuous here, so there's not much chance of Biggles missing us when he waffles along – if you see what I mean?'

'We shall be just as conspicuous to von Stalhein, or some blighter in that Hurricane of yours, if he should come along first,' said Algy gloomily. 'Getting the tank hit was a dirty slice of luck. It was rotten luck that von Stalhein should roll up just when he did, if it comes to that. It shook me to see him step out of that Mosquito. I wonder what he's doing out here?'

'I heard him shouting something about Canton,' offered Bertie.

'Yes. I suppose that was it. Judging from what he said to Odenski, his secret service had reported that Canton was in jail. That put him in a flap no doubt, because having seen Canton take off on a non-stop run to the oasis, he'd wonder how it could have happened. Maybe he dashed out to El Asile to check up. Had he been five minutes later we shouldn't be in this mess.'

'Had he been five minutes earlier we shouldn't have got off. That's how it goes, old boy, that's how it goes,' returned Bertie philosophically. 'Queer how chilly it gets in these places after sundown.'

'The air, it is so dry,' put in Emile. 'To keep warm, lie down and cover the body with sand. Always the sand stays warm.'

'I'm not going to make a rabbit of myself and get my ears full of the beastly stuff,' declared Bertie.

After that nobody spoke for some time. They just sat, in a silence that was profound, waiting for the morning light.

It was Emile who broke the spell. He appeared to be asleep, but suddenly he started and scrambled to his feet. 'Alas!' he exclaimed in a hollow voice. 'Now we shall have grief. *Voila!*'

Staring across the moonlit wilderness in the direction in which the lad was pointing, Algy saw what appeared to be a sinuous shadow moving towards them. 'What on earth is that?' he asked sharply.

'Arabs,' answered Emile. 'Only Tuareg would come here. Some are good. Some are bad. They fear no one.'

'Then let's hope these are some of the good boys,' murmured Bertie.

Nothing could be done. As the shadow drew nearer, Algy saw that it was composed of camels, each with a muffled rider. There were, he estimated, not fewer than fifty of them. Soft-padded feet made an eerie sound on the sand as the Arabs advanced. It was like no other sound he had ever heard. It was the only sound. There was something unnerving about the deliberate, silent approach. That the machine had been seen was obvious. There was nothing surprising about that. The Douglas, the only object on miles of flat desert, was as conspicuous as a beetle on a sheet of white paper. The watchful eyes of the Tuareg must have spotted it from a great distance.

As the riders drew near, the majority split into two lines, which, moving in opposite directions, quickly encircled the aircraft and its crew. A few came on to where the white men stood waiting. There was something frightening, but at the same time impressive, about the upright, confident bearing of these warriors of the wilderness.

'Can you speak their language?' Algy asked Emile anxiously.

'Some of it, I think. We shall see,' was the reply.

'If these are the fellows who were shot up at El Asile when they tried to get a drink, I should say we've had it,' observed Bertie calmly. 'We couldn't blame them for knocking us off.'

Algy, who had forgotten the incident, wished Bertie hadn't mentioned it. The sense of the remark was all too evident.

The Arabs closed up, presenting a striking spectacle, yet at the same time creating a sensation of unreality. In the moonlight the camels and their riders looked enormous. Every man, Algy noticed with dismay, carried a rifle and a lance.

Even after the camels had been brought to a halt, forming a semicircle before the white men, the sinister silence persisted. Looking up, all Algy could see was a pair of dark eyes above the veil that every man wore. Not being able to speak induced an unpleasant feeling of helplessness.

It was Emile who spoke first. What he said, neither Algy nor Bertie knew, of course. At all events, he received an answer, which was something; and for a little while a laconic conversation in gutteral tones was carried on. Then Emile turned to Algy and said, simply: 'They are going to kill us because the white men in the valley refused them water and shot two of their warriors.'

To Algy this information came as a shock, because as far as actions were concerned the Tuareg had shown no signs of hostility or violence. 'Tell them,' he told Emile, 'that we are enemies of the men in the valley, who are thieves and murderers. The Government has sent us here to seize them and take them away. When these men have gone the

Tuareg will always be able to take as much water as they want.'

This message Emile passed on. It received a dubious reception. There was some more talking, and again Emile translated. 'The Tuareg say they are on their way to the oasis to kill these men themselves.'

'Tell them that if they do that there will be trouble,' requested Algy. 'French soldiers are on their way to capture these men and take them to prison. Let the Tuareg wait. If they kill us the soldiers will know of it and the water in the valley will be destroyed.'

Emile conveyed the message. Another argument followed, in which there seemed to be some difference of opinion between the Tuareg themselves.

'They say,' said Emile, 'that if they spare our lives we will fetch soldiers to punish them for attacking the oasis.'

'Tell them that if they spare our lives they will be rewarded. They can help the soldiers when they come. If they kill us it is certain that war will be made on them and the oasis destroyed, which would be a bad thing for all Arabs.'

There was more talking.

At length Emile shrugged his expressive shoulders. Said he: 'It is no use, *monsieur*. They have sworn death to the men in the valley for the blood they have shed, and nothing shall stop them. So that we shall not give warning we must go with them. If we fight on their side it will prove we are enemies of the men in the valley.'

'Tell them we cannot move the aeroplane. We will stay here. Why, do they think, are we sitting here in the desert?'

'This I have told them, but they will not believe it.'

'Can't blame 'em,' put in Bertie. 'We must admit these lads have a jolly good argument, having had two of their chaps shot, and all the rest of it.'

Algy made up his mind quickly. If it was a question of being shot or going with them, obviously, it was better to go with them. 'Tell them,' he told Emile, 'that we will go with them, for it was our purpose, with the aid of soldiers, to make prisoners of the men in the valley.'

Actually, of course, he saw clearly enough that this was not really a matter of choice. Whatever happened the Tuareg would not go on and leave them to warn – as they would suppose was possible – either the French post at Insalah or the men at El Asile. He had a vague hope that before the Arabs could attack, something would happen to prevent it. Biggles, he was sure, having got Marcel's message, would by this time be on the way, and he would not be likely to come alone.

There was no more talking. The Arabs closed up in readiness to move off. Emile said they must go with them. There were no spare camels, so they would have to walk. The Tuareg, he added bitterly, had no fear that they would try to run away.

The return journey to El Asile began, with the Douglas, looking pathetically lonely and forlorn, standing where it was grounded. As near as he could judge Algy reckoned they had about ten miles to go. He was by no means sure, because he had been too occupied with the petrol trouble to pay attention to distance. Anyhow, they had a long walk in front of them, there was no doubt about that.

In actual practice it seemed interminable. There was only one redeeming feature. The cool night air was invigorating, and none of them suffered any particular fatigue. If they had had bad luck, thought Algy on reflection, it had, as usual, been counterbalanced by good, in that Emile had thought fit to stow himself in the machine. He hated to think of what would have happened had he and Bertie found themselves beset by the Tuareg without any means of speaking with them.

The march was maintained in silence. The only sound was the soft padding of the camels, so supercilious in expression and so distinctive in aroma. The quaint thought struck him that they had started the night with the latest form of transport, and were ending it with what was probably one of the oldest. The going became harder as the sand gave way to rock, through which the riders threaded as they sought the easiest route. Hills on either side told Algy that they were drawing near to their objective.

He did not trouble to wonder what was likely to happen if the attack developed into a serious battle, as it might, for the White Prophets were armed and would certainly fight. Whichever side won, their plight, he was sure, would be an unpleasant one. The Prophets, on their part, would give them short shrift if they caught them. What the Tuareg would do if they won was a matter for conjecture, but as it could not be worse it appeared to be the lesser of the two evils. He hoped, therefore, that the Arabs would win. They were obviously relying on a surprise attack to achieve this, and this reminded him of the two sentries that had been posted. Were the Tuareg aware of this, he wondered? If not, the onset was likely to fail. As he did not want this to happen, the Arabs, he thought, should be warned. Such a warning would prove which side they were on. Touching Emile on the arm, he whispered the suggestion.

Emile hurried forward, and having gained the leader's attention spoke to him quietly for a little while. Then he returned to his place. 'The information was well received,' he breathed. 'The Tuareg now think better of us.'

It was getting on towards dawn, with the moon an enormous orange disc balanced on the horizon, when the party came to a halt. Without a sound the Arabs 'couched' their camels and dismounted. Not a word was spoken. To Algy this was a wonderful example of discipline among men to whom orthodox military training was unknown.

He could not imagine white troops behaving in the same way. But then, he pondered, here silence was everything. In the thin, dry air the slightest sound was amplified a hundred times.

Algy, Bertie, and Emile, stood watching while preparations for the attack were made. No one took any notice of them. They might not have existed. In small parties the Arabs departed like ghostly shapes to merge into the rocks ahead. At last only a few remained, in charge of the camels.

It is not to be supposed that Algy watched these preparations without misgivings. Putting aside the characters of the men in the valley, they were, after all, white men. They were going to be attacked, and probably killed. Some of them, certainly, would be killed. That this state of affairs was due to their own folly was true, but it did not alter the fact. Wherefore he felt uncomfortable. But he did not see what they could do. The attack would be launched whatever they did, anyway. Anything they did to frustrate it, even a remonstrance, would be taken by the Arabs as a hostile action, with disastrous results for them. It came to this. He would have warned the men in the valley had it been possible; but it was illogical to throw his life away in a futile attempt to save men who, given the opportunity, would kill him without the slightest compunction. Von Stalhein had, in fact, tried to kill him. So Algy did nothing. He merely sat on a convenient rock and waited for what might befall. There Bertie and Emile joined him. There was nothing to say, so nothing was said.

The waiting became a strain. The silence, the utter absence of sound, was a sensation in itself, something not of this world with its busy communities, but of the great empty spaces of the universe.

It ended abruptly just as the first glow of the false dawn smudged the eastern sky with a glow of pale pink. Then came the dawn wind, breathing across the desert. A ray of light shone upwards, and with it came a gunshot, so clear, so loud, that Algy's nerves twitched like a steel spring suddenly released. The shot was followed by a volley.

Algy looked at Bertie. 'There they go,' he said softly.

15

THE SUN DICTATES

The onset in the valley, once launched, developed quickly into a battle of some intensity, the noise of which made further silence on the part of Algy and Bertie unnecessary. The roll of musketry became almost continuous. Occasionally it was punctuated by a shout – from one of the white defenders, Algy thought. The Tuareg camel guards stood like statues beside their beasts, apparently not in the least concerned by what was going on.

'I didn't realize we were so close to the valley,' Algy told Bertie. 'It must be just over that next ridge.'

'If Biggles or any of them happen to arrive in the middle of this fuss they'll think we're putting up a jolly good show,' remarked Bertie.

Algy had been thinking the same thing. He wondered what would happen if Biggles did come, because should his intention be to land there was only one place, and that was in the valley itself. All round it the ground was broken, more rock than sand, between low hills deeply fissured.

There was no indication of how the conflict was going, although when a machine gun, or an automatic weapon of some sort, opened up, Bertie observed, inconsequentially: 'I'll bet the old Tuareg won't think much of that.'

Algy did not answer. He jumped up as another, an even more significant sound, became audible above the din of war. It was the roar of aircraft motors. He assumed, naturally, that it was Biggles, forgetting for a moment that the enemy had aircraft. He was not a little startled when a Mosquito flashed into view, not from the direction he expected, but from the valley. So low was it that he ducked, thinking the wheels, which were still down, were going to hit the rocks, in which case the machine must have crashed on top of them. The undercarriage missed the rocks by inches, and in a few seconds the aircraft was out of sight beyond some rising ground, going, as Bertie remarked, coarsely but aptly, like a bat out of hell.

'That'll be von Stalhein, getting out,' said Algy. 'Trust him. Well, he may have a shock when he gets home – that's if he's going to the Plaine de la Crau.'

The shooting was by this time tending to become sporadic. Presently smoke, coal-black smoke, began to coil sluggishly into the blue sky. Some of it was caught in a down draught and drawn back into the valley.

'That's oil,' declared Algy. 'The Tuareg have either set the dump on fire or the machines.'

'The smoke's coming from the *nullah* where they're kept, anyhow,' confirmed Bertie.

A few more shots were fired, and then the battle slowly fizzled out. The Tuareg warriors began to drift back in small parties, some limping, a few helping others apparently wounded. They went to their camels and stood waiting. Few were missing, Algy thought. When, after an interval, no more appeared, the Arabs mounted quietly and rode away. There was still no talking, nor did they display any signs of emotion to suggest how things had gone with them.

Bertie sprang up. 'By Jove! They're going to leave us here!'

'They might have done worse than that,' replied Algy. 'I suppose they don't want to clutter themselves up with us.'

'But I say, old boy, we'll never find our way back to the machine!' declared Bertie.

'We should be crazy to try, particularly as we have no water,' answered Algy. 'The only water is in the valley, and I'm staying near it. We couldn't last twenty-four hours without a drink.'

'Then we'd better have a look at what's happened,' opined Bertie.

They all moved forward to the ridge that cut off their view, and below which, as they presently discovered, a rocky bank fell steeply into the valley perhaps a hundred feet below. Reaching it first, Algy looked over – carelessly, as he realized an instant later when a bullet smashed against a rock unpleasantly close.

'They're not all dead, anyhow,' said Bertie, unnecessarily.

Algy had ducked back under cover. 'No. And if they keep that sort of thing up we're in a mess.'

'Why?'

'We can't just sit here. We've got to get to water.'

Bertie looked perplexed. 'How dashed awkward. If we stay here we frizzle. If we try to get to the trough we shall be shot. But there is this about it, laddie; if their machines have been set on fire the blighters can't get away.'

'Neither can we.'

'They'll be stuck here – absolutely pegged down by the ears, and all that.'

'That doesn't help us.'

'Too true, old boy, too true. Well, what are we going to do about it?' Bertie polished his eyeglass vigorously. 'I want a drink.'

'If you stick your head over that ridge what you'll get is a bullet.'

'We shall have to find out what's happened in the valley.'

'Just a minute.' Algy crawled a little way and peeped cautiously between two rocks. Dimly through the drifting smoke he could see several bodies lying about, both brown and white. There was nobody moving, from which he assumed that the survivors of the attack had taken refuge in the buildings. He returned to the others. 'Nothing much to see,' he announced. 'The Prophets have gone into cover. I don't suppose they realize that the Tuareg have gone. I hope they go on thinking that, because if they knew we were here by ourselves they'd soon be after us.'

'Then the thing is to keep them guessing until Biggles or Joudrier comes to winkle them out,' suggested Bertie.

'That's all very fine, but we can't last a day without water.'

'If we bang off at them every time they try to get to the well, they won't get a drink, either.'

'As I said before, that won't quench our thirst. In any case, I shouldn't be able to do much execution with my pistol. That's the only weapon we've got.'

'Could we make a rush and grab the rifles of some of the blokes who have gone for a Burton?'

Algy looked doubtful. 'This is no place to stop a bullet. My inclination is to stay under cover and let them make the first move. If they caught sight of us they might guess the Tuareg have gone.'

'Okay, old boy. Just as you like,' agreed Bertie. 'We'll wait for Biggles to roll up.'

There was a long lull in the conversation, and as the sun was now striking down with considerable force they moved a little way to a bluff, on one side of which there was still a narrow strip of shade.

'We've no hope of getting out of this until Biggles comes,' resumed Algy, who had been giving some thought to the matter. 'What worries me is, what is he going to do when he gets here? The only possible landing-place is in the valley, and if he goes down there he's liable to be shot before he can get an idea of what's happening.'

'By Jove! You're absolutely right!' returned Bertie, looking alarmed. 'We mustn't let that happen.'

'I've been thinking about it,' went on Algy. 'As far as I can see the best thing we can do is lie doggo until we hear him coming, then sprint to the top of one of these hills and wave a shirt or something. If he spots us up here he'll realize there's something wrong.'

'True enough,' conceded Bertie.

Again the conversation languished while the sun climbed to its zenith and tormented the earth with its merciless rays. The shadow of the bluff dwindled, and by the time the sun was immediately overhead there was no shade left. There was no shade anywhere. Algy, reluctant to be the first to complain, stuck it for as long as he could, but at length finding the position no longer endurable, was forced to say: 'This is no use. I'm being cooked alive. This infernal sun will flay us if we stay here.'

'I'm all dried up,' declared Bertie. 'As you say, laddie, it's no use. We shall have to shift. Anything is better than this.'

They got up, and after walking a little way were fortunate to find a little cavity into which the sun had not yet penetrated. In this they crouched. No one mentioned water, although each knew that the others must be suffering considerably from thirst. Bertie's remark about being dried up was becoming literally true.

More time passed, with the sun flaming its daily journey across the sky. Its rays found the cavity and bombarded it with lances of fire.

'A nasty thought has just occurred to me,' said Algy, after a while.

'What is it?' Bertie spoke with difficulty through parched lips.

'Biggles might be at Insalah, waiting for us.'

'Why should he wait?'

'He might think, knowing we're here, that if he came over he might start something – make things more difficult for us to get away.'

Bertie nodded. 'I never thought of that. In that case it's no use sitting here.'

But still they sat for a little while, not knowing what else to do. At last Algy got up. 'I'm going to see if I can find a cave or something. We've got to get out of this sun, or we shan't last till nightfall. Personally, I'd risk anything for a drink.'

Keeping well back from the ridge, they went on again for some little way. The sun was now falling towards the west, and slim black shadows were beginning to reappear; but the ground in such places, having been exposed to the sun, was too hot to sit on.

'If we had rifles,' said Bertie, 'I'd risk an attack on the valley. Or we could make a diversion while someone grabbed some water.'

'We haven't any rifles,' rejoined Algy impatiently.

Emile, who up to now had taken no part in the conversation, went off to do some scouting on his own account. When he returned he had this to say. He had been along to the end of the valley. There were, he stated, some casualties lying near the mouth of the ravine where the machines had been parked. There were rifles lying near them. There was also a fair amount of smoke, perhaps enough to cover them while they fetched the rifles. He was willing to try for the rifles.

'We'll all go,' declared Algy. 'Just a minute.' He snapped a shot from his automatic into the valley. 'Just to make 'em think the Tuareg are still here and encourage them to stay indoors,' he explained.

Little dreaming of the revelations that were to be the outcome of their sortie, they started moving along the side of the valley, keeping more or less parallel with it but well below the danger line of the ridge. In doing this they made their first discovery. It was not a nice one. It was the body of a white man, apparently one of the sentries. Unfortunately his rifle and cartridges were not there. The Tuareg, Emil thought, would take them, for in the desert a high price is put upon such things.

They carried on, and after a while found a place from which a reasonably safe reconnaissance of their objective could be made. A buttress of rock intervened between them, and that part of the valley where the buildings stood. Here again the spectacle was one of tragedy. Near the entrance to the ravine, lying as they had fallen, were several bodies. There were two Arabs. Here the weapons had not been collected; they lay beside their owners, who would never need them again. The scene in the ravine itself was one of devastation. The whole place had been burnt out, and was still smoking. Through the murk could be seen the metal skeletons of the aircraft.

'By the way, the place doesn't seem to be what you might call swarming with ibex,' remarked Bertie.

'I'd say they were all liquidated long ago,' replied Algy.

He looked for some time at the bodies. 'Let's get what we came for and clear out,' he said suddenly. 'This is turning out to be a nastier affair than I expected. Thank heavens the sun will soon be behind those hills. The worst of the heat is over, but we've got to have water.'

Bertie touched him on the arm and pointed. 'That looks mighty like Odenski lying over there.'

Algy looked. And as he stared he thought he saw the body move slightly. 'Whoever it is he's still alive. We'd better go and see. Watch out for treachery.'

They made their way cautiously to the object of their inquiry, collecting rifles and ammunition as they went.

'It is Odenski,' said Bertie. 'He and the others must have gone down trying to keep the Arabs out of the ravine.'

The prostrate man may have heard the sound of voices, for, with an obvious effort, he half-raised his head. 'Water,' he pleaded weakly. 'Water.'

Algy hurried forward. 'What's the trouble, Odenski?'

'Water. Give me water.'

It was obvious to Algy that the man was in a bad way. With a thrill of horror he realized that he must have been lying there all day. His own men had left him there, or had not troubled to look for him. Such brutal behaviour filled Algy with anger.

'Water,' pleaded Odenski.

'I haven't any,' answered Algy. He made a quick examination. 'Got it in the stomach,' he told Bertie in a soft aside. 'He hasn't a hope.'

'The rats. The dirty rats.' Odenski seemed to be muttering to himself.

'They've gone,' said Algy, thinking, naturally, that he meant the Tuareg.

'Save themselves...that's all they cared.' The wounded man's mind was wandering towards that place from which there is no return.

Algy dropped on one knee, frowning. 'Who are you talking about?'

'Von Stalhein and Groot.'

'You mean – they left you?'

'Von Stalhein shot me.'

'*Shot* you!' This was something Algy did not expect. Furrows of doubt and incredulity creased his forehead. 'But why should they shoot you?'

Anger seemed to give the wounded man fresh strength. 'I saw them creep off towards the ravine. Left us to hold the Arabs while they got out, the curs. I went after them. Von Stalhein told me to get back. The plane would only carry two, he said. I told him he was yellow. Then he pulled a gun and plugged me. Went off with Groot...left me here. Water...get me water.'

'Why didn't your men come?' asked Algy wrathfully.

'They did...for the keys...of the canteen,' was the shocking answer.

The face that Algy turned to Bertie was pale and drawn with indignation. 'This is awful. We must get this wretched fellow a drink. He hasn't much longer. Hark!'

From the buildings round the corner came the sound of voices raised in ribald song. 'Could you believe that?' he said through his teeth. 'They found Odenski, took the keys of the canteen, and left him here. Now they're all drunk. No wonder they didn't bother with us. What a pack of swine they must be! Let's try to get some water.'

'The well is up near the palms,' volunteered Bertie.

Algy ran forward to the buttress and looked round the end. Evening shadows were now softening the picture, but he could see two or three bodies lying near the palms. There was no movement anywhere. 'I think we might do it,' he said. 'It's worth risking.'

'I know where the can is kept,' said Emile, and before anyone could stop him he was racing, bending low, towards the palms.

Algy dropped on one knee, loaded his rifle quickly, brought it to the ready and waited. 'Shoot if you see anything move,' he told Bertie tersely.

The fact that Emile was not shot at until he was well on his way back may have been partly due to a diversion which, while not unexpected, coming when it did had an almost demoralizing effect. With a roar a Mosquito came tearing up the valley. Algy was torn between looking at it and at Emile, who finished his mad dash with bullets kicking up the sand at his feet. He stuck to the can of water he carried, and panting, held it out to Algy.

Algy hastened to Odenski, but stopped suddenly. 'Too late,' he said. 'He's gone.'

'Put the water in a safe place where we can get at it,' suggested Algy practically.

After they had all had a quick drink Algy complied. But he was now more concerned with the aircraft, which he had recognized as Biggles' machine. Its arrival reintroduced the problem that had been worrying him for some time. Not that there was anything he could do. It was no use waving and expecting to be seen. In the end he adhered to the original plan. As the machine came in to land, as he expected it would, he, Bertie, and Emile opened a brisk fire on the canteen, from which, from some reason not then apparent, there came little answering fire. The one or two shots that were fired had no effect.

The Mosquito touched down in the middle of the valley, its nose pointing in the direction of the ravine. Algy, throwing discretion to the winds, raced towards it, waving frantically. That he had been seen was soon evident, for there was a burst of throttle and the Mosquito came on, tail up.

The noise alone must by now have given Biggles an idea of what was happening, for Bertie and Emile were shooting at the canteen as fast as they could load. The fact that they were there at all must have told Biggles something, too. Anyway, in response to Algy's furious beckoning Biggles ran the machine on until it was behind the buttress; then, followed by Ginger, he jumped down and ran for cover.

Wonder was written all over his face. He glanced at the smoking wreckage in the ravine and at the bodies lying about, before his eyes came to rest on Algy. 'What in thunder is going on here?' he rapped out.

'You might well ask,' retorted Algy. 'We're having a great time.'

'I can see that,' answered Biggles grimly. 'I don't know that Joudrier is going to be too pleased about this when he gets here.'

'We didn't start it, old boy,' protested Bertie.

'Who did?'

'A bunch of Arabs mopped the place up,' informed Bertie. 'We told them not to, the blighters, but they wouldn't take any notice of us – would they, Algy?'

Algy shook his head. 'No notice at all.'

'You'd better put me wise so that I shall know where I am when Joudrier comes,' requested Biggles. 'It looks to me as if you've stolen his party.'

'You can bet your sweet life we didn't steal it from choice,' averred Algy warmly.

Then he told Biggles all about it.

It was nearly dark by the time he had finished. Even before that they could hear aircraft in the distance.

Marcel's Morane was the first to appear, although it was soon followed by a Dakota which apparently it had escorted. Marcel dived, tore up the valley, came round in a climbing turn and then side-slipped in. Before his wheels had touched the Dakota had appeared, and the air vibrated with the roar of engines.

'This looks like the beginning of the end,' remarked Biggles, who stood watching.

'Shouldn't we try to warn them that they're liable to be shot at?' queried Ginger.

'Somehow I don't think there'll be much shooting,' answered Biggles. 'When these dud Prophets see what they're up against they'll throw in the towel. They must know that without transport they can't get away, and it isn't going to make their case any better if they shoot a policeman.'

It fell out much as Biggles predicted. When Marcel landed he saw the Mosquito and taxied on to it. The Dakota followed, slowly, shedding a surprisingly powerful force of gendarmes. It was clear that Joudrier was taking no risks.

From all sides the police closed in on the building. Those who were already there joined in the operation, to see the finish, although this bore little resemblance to what might have been imagined. Only one or two shots were fired. One gendarme was wounded in the thigh. He was the only casualty.

When the final rush was made on the canteen an extraordinary spectacle greeted the eyes of the spectators. For a minute Joudrier was speechless with bewilderment. 'And we thought this was a religious house!' cried he, throwing up his hands. His indignation was understandable. Of the nine survivors of the Tuareg attack not one was sober. Five were on the floor, completely out. Bottles and glasses lay about to bear witness to the fantastic orgy that had taken place.

'What a mob,' breathed Biggles. 'Heavens above, what a mob! When a gang of crooks breaks up it usually goes to pieces, but I never saw anything like this.'

Joudrier came over. 'Tonight we stay here,' he said. 'Tomorrow we will clean up.'

'We'll stay for the performance,' answered Biggles. 'You're welcome to the job. I'm still hoping to find the gold for our friends in Australia.' He turned to Bertie. 'You know your way about. Find us somewhere to sleep.'

16

WHERE THE TRAILS ENDED

The following day saw the end of El Asile as a white settlement, religious or otherwise. Captain Joudrier, as the senior French official, took charge, with Marcel as his assistant, so Biggles and his friends remained really as spectators. They needed a rest, for since the case had opened they had covered a lot of ground, as Biggles had predicted would happen when big criminal enterprises were conducted on wings.

The dead 'Prophets' were buried alongside the Tuareg who had died in pursuit of vengeance. The surviving white men, in handcuffs, were loaded into the Dakota under an armed guard and flown to Algiers. Later they were taken to Paris, where they were dealt with according to their misdeeds. As so often happens, these miserable men turned on each other at the finish, hoping by this to get a lighter sentence, with the result that there was no dearth of evidence to secure their conviction.

Biggles' chief interest – indeed, his only remaining interest – in El Asile now was the recovery of the Australian gold which he was convinced was there. A good deal of mystery still surrounded this gold. No one had seen a particle of it. There was no doubt whatever in Biggles' mind that the Count's gang had been responsible for the robbery, but belief was not proof, and proof was what a court of law would demand. One ounce of the gold would be enough. An assayer would soon determine where it came from. But none could be found. The only material known to have been carried by air was the blackish powder described as fertilizer. A fair quantity of this had been found at the Villa Hirondelle. There was some in the Douglas that Algy had put down in the desert.

Biggles had given a lot of thought to this puzzling factor. He had not yet had an opportunity of examining the stuff, and was pleased when Joudrier called him to say that a further quantity had been discovered and he would like an opinion on it.

They all went to the isolated stone building, the original building erected by Monsieur Bourdau, where the discovery had been made. Biggles had not so far been inside this because there had been some difficulty in getting it open. As a matter of detail it turned out to be the only room about which there was anything remarkable, the other buildings comprising workshops and living accommodation.

The large chamber into which Joudrier now led the way contained equipment which at first glance appeared to have no possible purpose at a desert oasis. It was something between a foundry and a laboratory. There was a long bench on which stood a small furnace fed by a gas cylinder on the floor. Scattered about were porcelain dishes, crucible tongs, and other miscellaneous utensils commonly associated with such things. Flush against the wall were two large slate bins, or troughs, containing liquid. Beside these were several straw-covered carboys, some containing liquid, some empty. On a table was a box containing white powder. Finally, on the floor there were several small jute bags containing what, according to the name printed boldly on the outside, was fertilizer. Some empty bags lay nearby. There were other things, but these need not be described. The air in the room was heavy with an acrid smell which reminded Ginger of chlorine.

All these things Biggles examined with a curious expression on his face. 'Well, well,' he said softly.

'Emile told me that Odenski was a chemist. He acted as a doctor when one was needed,' said Bertie. 'It looks as if this is where he amused himself in his spare time.'

'Amused himself?' Biggles smiled. 'This is where he worked. And this outfit was his surgery. The stuff isn't fertilizer, of course, although it might get by people who don't know what we know. Let's see if we can find out what it really is.' He turned to Joudrier. 'With your permission, Monsieur le Capitaine, I will try an experiment, one that I once saw demonstrated in the laboratory at school when I was a boy. I hope I haven't forgotten the details.'

In silence, watched by the others, he lit the jet of the furnace and turned the burner low. Then, using crucible tongs, he filled a porcelain dish with some of the liquid contained in one of the troughs. This he stood on the burner.

'What is that liquid?' asked Ginger.

'Never interrupt a trick in the middle,' said Biggles seriously. Then he smiled. 'Knowing that you suffer from impatience, I'd better tell you. If my guess is right, most of it is gold.'

Even Joudrier looked astonished, and more than slightly sceptical at this reply.

No one spoke as Biggles added to the liquid some of the white powder from the box.

'What's that stuff?' Ginger wanted to know.

'There's no name on it, but if this set-up is what I take it to be, it should be iron sulphate,' answered Biggles. 'Watch. Ah-ha.' A note of triumph crept into his voice.

Peering forward, the spectators saw a dark brown powder appear at the bottom of the dish.

'What's that?' demanded Ginger.

'Fertilizer,' returned Biggles sarcastically. 'Don't be in a hurry.' He poured the liquid off, returned the dish to the furnace and turned up the flame. The powder settled down into a small gleaming yellow disc. This he poured on the bench. 'You needn't ask me what that is,' he bantered, glancing at Ginger.

'Gold!'

'Quite right. The stuff they dig out of the ground at Barula Creek.'

'Well, blow me down!' gasped Bertie.

'One never knows when the simple chemistry one learns at school is going to be useful,' said Biggles. His smile broadened. 'A mixture of nitric and muriatic acids, boiled, is one of the few things that will dissolve gold. I imagine those carboys over there contain acid. Not many people would recognize gold in its liquid form; but as it wouldn't be easy to handle like that, our prophetic friends turned it into a substance that might easily pass for the fertilizer known as basic slag. Add sulphate of iron to the liquid, and the gold is precipitated – but you saw what happened. When I heated the precipitate it returned to its original form of metallic gold.' He tossed the apparatus on the bench.

'It's all plain enough now,' he went on, lighting a cigarette. 'Gold is controlled, checked and double-checked by every country in the world. Stolen gold, as freight, is red hot – that is, if it's in its usual form, which anyone can recognize. A machine carrying it wouldn't dare to land at an airport. Indeed, a machine landing anywhere would find a cargo of gold hard to explain. The same risk would be present with surface craft. The Count hit upon the scheme of making it unrecognizable; or it may have been

Odenski's idea. It was a simple trick. Remember, it was not only the Count who was handling the stuff. Black-market merchants, like the Roumanians who were mentioned, were buying it from him. They, too, would have to transport it, and no doubt they preferred it in the form of dust rather than ingots. Well, there it is. Now we know the answers. The gold will have to be collected and sent back to where it belongs.' Biggles turned to Joudrier. 'If it's all the same to you I think I'll be moving off now. You know where to find me if you want me.'

'What about the Count and von Stalhein?' asked Algy.

'I'm hoping that von Stalhein and Groot, who was with him, will have landed at the Plaine de la Crau, in which case they would find Joudrier's men waiting to receive them. As for the Count – well, he might be anywhere by now, and I'm not going to spend the rest of my life looking for him. We shall hear of him again, no doubt. For the time being I'm satisfied that the gang has been broken up.'

Bertie chose this moment to chuckle. 'The Count paid me jolly well for the short time I worked for him,' he averred, cheerfully.

'Oh. And what did he pay you?' inquired Biggles.

'He gave me a hundred thousand franc notes.' Bertie's hand dived into his pocket, and he displayed the wad with a flourish.

Joudrier held out a hand. 'Let me look at those,' he requested. He looked. 'Forgeries,' he said calmly, and put them in his own pocket. 'They can go on the fire.'

Everyone burst out laughing at the expression on Bertie's face.

'Here, I say, that's a bit tough!' he cried indignantly.

Raising a warning finger, Joudrier went on. '*Attendez, monsieur*. There is reason to think that this man who calls himself Count von Horndorf is Jacob Theller, the master printer, who in the war forged notes for Hitler for use in the countries he occupied. We found many of these notes on the people we arrested at the Villa Hirondelle. Always we have had these bad notes in France to make the changing of money difficult. We did not know where they came from. In the safe at the Villa Hirondelle there were old letters addressed to Jacob Theller. By description the man is the same.'

'Well, all I can say is, after all my honest sweat, I call that a pretty low trick,' said Bertie disgustedly. 'Is nobody honest in this world?'

There was more laughter as the party broke up.

Marcel elected to remain at the oasis with Joudrier until everything had been dealt with, but promised to run over to Gatwick at the first opportunity. Soon afterwards, taking Ginger with him, Biggles got into the Mosquito and headed north for home, leaving Algy and Bertie to follow in the Dakota when it returned to pick up Joudrier and his men. Biggles told them they could take a day or two off in the South of France, where Algy had some business to clear up; they could then fly home in the Auster that was still at Nice.

The final records of the strange case of the White Prophets were only completed over a period of time.

In the matter of von Stalhein, Biggles was disappointed to learn, when he reached France, that the calculating German had managed to evade capture by employing the same callous methods that had got him out of trouble on more than one occasion. The Mosquito, as Biggles expected, had gone straight to the Plaine de la Crau, and had actually landed there. Joudrier's men were waiting. It so happened that, either by accident or by the design of his wily companion, Groot had got out first. Not realizing that anyone else was in the machine, the gendarmes had made a rush at him. Groot had pulled a gun and tried to fight his way back to the machine, and in this he might have succeeded had von Stalhein waited for him. But the aircraft had taken off again. Groot, in his fury, had shot and wounded a gendarme, and was thereupon shot dead. The Mosquito was never seen again. What happened to it became a matter for surmise, but in view of what Algy had overheard about the headquarters of the gang being moved to behind the Iron Curtain, Biggles was of the opinion that von Stalhein had found refuge there.

The Count may have headed for the same sanctuary, but his fate, revealed afterwards, was definite. Weeks later some climbers in the Swiss Alps came upon the wreckage of an aircraft that had flown into the side of a mountain, either as a result of inefficient pilotage or bad weather. There were two bodies. Lying beside them was a valise that concussion had burst open. One of the bodies was identified as that of Jacob Theller, long wanted by the police for his wartime activities. His pilot, from the papers he carried, was one Luis Leguez, a Mexican ex-gangster of Chicago, who had been 'put on the spot' by his associates there. What was more important than the bodies were the contents of the valise. It had been packed with new currency notes of several nationalities; more important still, the plates from which they had been engraved were there. These were, of course, destroyed, and a menace that had long embarrassed European banks was removed for all time. On closer examination by the police the valise was found to have a false bottom. In this was a wonderful collection of precious stones which, on being identified, disclosed the robberies that the Count and his gang had engineered.

As Biggles remarked when he heard this news, with so much wealth available it was no matter for wonder that the Count was able to finance an air organization on such an ambitious scale. He must have known there was a limit to how far he could go in the distribution of spurious notes, so he had engaged himself in turning them into the universally recognized units of wealth – gold and precious stones.

Emile, by his behaviour at El Asile, had already in effect turned King's Evidence, so no charge was preferred against him. He had to rejoin his regiment, but the influence of Captain Joudrier, backed by Biggles, soon secured for him what, as a result of his brief association with aircraft, he now wanted, which was to be a military pilot. On the completion of his training he was posted to North Africa, a location for which his desert experience made him eminently suitable.

One final curious fact emerged from the case, as Biggles pointed out when the matter was discussed at leisure. Monsieur Bourdau, who had spent a fortune in a genuine attempt to save the ibex, had, although fortunately he did not know it, provided the means of their extinction. Not one survived the occupation of the oasis. Some, after persistent persecution, may have wandered away to safer pastures; but the majority must have fallen to the rifles of the meat-hungry adventurers who called themselves the White Prophets.

Captain W E Johns

Biggles and the Missing Millionaire

Biggles and his friends are given a seemingly impossible task when they are asked to locate the luxury yacht, *Cordelia,* and its master. The five-hundred-ton vessel – owned by troubled international financier Otto Brandt – simply slipped her mooring one night and sailed off into obscurity on the high seas. The team's mission is further complicated by a young Italian who is bent on revenge.

Biggles and the Pirate Treasure and Other Stories

In this collection of short stories, Biggles and his team cover ground from London to the Indian Ocean in the course of their eventful investigations. In 'Biggles and the Pirate Treasure', they are asked to help their French counterparts locate pirate treasure buried hundreds of years before by a French pirate in Madagascar.

Each story is filled with adventure and daring and each case tests Biggles' skill and intelligence to the limit.

Captain W E Johns

Biggles Breaks the Silence

When Biggles is sent off on a mission to Antarctica to find the wreck of the *Starry Crown* and the treasure she was carrying, little does he know the risks he is taking. The dangers posed by shifting icebergs, polar ice and appalling weather conditions make his trip to Graham Land extremely hazardous. But his expedition is made even more perilous when he encounters a bunch of desperadoes who will stop at nothing to make sure Biggles and his men do not return.

Biggles Flies to Work

In this collection of short stories, Biggles and his Air Police find themselves involved in some unusual cases. Their adventures include the foiling of an escape from Dartmoor Prison, the recovery of a cache of valuable coins from a hiding place in Albania and discovering the story behind a diamond necklace found hanging from the top of a tree.

Captain W E Johns

Biggles of the Special Air Police

In 'The Black Gauntlet', Biggles is asked to work as a technical advisor on a film's air-combat shots and he uncovers the strange mystery of a black gauntlet sent to him anonymously, while, in 'The Ace of Spades', we see Biggles in action as a skilful fighter pilot.

In this selection of short stories, whatever the adventure, Biggles always wins through with a mixture of luck, ability and bravery.

Biggles Takes a Holiday

The rambling tale of a dying man leads Biggles and his team to the snake-infested jungles of South America. Their mission is to rescue former squadron member, Angus Mackail. In the sweltering heat of Paradise Valley, their friend is being used as a human guinea-pig by the tyrannical Doctor Liebgarten. But events take a turn for the worse when Biggles finds out that his old enemy, Eric von Stalhein, is lying in wait...

TITLES BY CAPTAIN W E JOHNS AVAILABLE DIRECT FROM HOUSE OF STRATUS

Quantity		£	$(US)	$(CAN)	€
☐	Biggles and the Missing Millionaire	6.99	12.95	19.95	13.50
☐	Biggles and the Pirate Treasure	6.99	12.95	19.95	13.50
☐	Biggles and the Plane that Disappeared	6.99	12.95	19.95	13.50
☐	Biggles Breaks the Silence	6.99	12.95	19.95	13.50
☐	Biggles Flies to Work	6.99	12.95	19.95	13.50
☐	Biggles Gets his Men	6.99	12.95	19.95	13.50
☐	Biggles Looks Back	6.99	12.95	19.95	13.50
☐	Biggles Makes Ends Meet	6.99	12.95	19.95	13.50
☐	Biggles of the Interpol	6.99	12.95	19.95	13.50
☐	Biggles of the Special Air Police	6.99	12.95	19.95	13.50

ALL HOUSE OF STRATUS BOOKS ARE AVAILABLE FROM GOOD BOOKSHOPS OR DIRECT FROM THE PUBLISHER:

Internet: **www.houseofstratus.com** including synopses and features.

Email: **sales@houseofstratus.com**
info@houseofstratus.com
(please quote author, title and credit card details.)

TITLES BY CAPTAIN W E JOHNS AVAILABLE DIRECT FROM HOUSE OF STRATUS

PAYMENT

Please tick currency you wish to use:

☐ £ (Sterling) ☐ $ (US) ☐ $ (CAN) ☐ € (Euros)

Allow for shipping costs charged per order plus an amount per book as set out in the tables below:

CURRENCY/DESTINATION

	£(Sterling)	$(US)	$(CAN)	€(Euros)
Cost per order				
UK	1.50	2.25	3.50	2.50
Europe	3.00	4.50	6.75	5.00
North America	3.00	3.50	5.25	5.00
Rest of World	3.00	4.50	6.75	5.00
Additional cost per book				
UK	0.50	0.75	1.15	0.85
Europe	1.00	1.50	2.25	1.70
North America	1.00	1.00	1.50	1.70
Rest of World	1.50	2.25	3.50	3.00

PLEASE SEND CHEQUE OR INTERNATIONAL MONEY ORDER
payable to: HOUSE OF STRATUS LTD or HOUSE OF STRATUS INC. or card payment as indicated

STERLING EXAMPLE

Cost of book(s):. . . . . Example: 3 x books at £6.99 each: £20.97
Cost of order: . . . . Example: £1.50 (Delivery to UK address)
Additional cost per book:. . . . . Example: 3 x £0.50: £1.50
Order total including shipping:. . . . . Example: £23.97

VISA, MASTERCARD, SWITCH, AMEX:

☐☐☐☐☐☐☐☐☐☐☐☐☐☐☐☐☐☐☐☐

Issue number (Switch only):

☐☐☐

Start Date: ☐☐/☐☐

Expiry Date: ☐☐/☐☐

Signature: ____________________

NAME: ____________________

ADDRESS: ____________________

COUNTRY: ____________________

ZIP/POSTCODE: ____________________

Please allow 28 days for delivery. Despatch normally within 48 hours.

Prices subject to change without notice.
Please tick box if you do not wish to receive any additional information. ☐

House of Stratus publishes many other titles in this genre; please check our website (**www.houseofstratus.com**) for more details.